KHCC

Books should be returned or renewed by the last date above. Renew by phone **03000 41 31 31** or online *www.kent.gov.uk/libs*

Guardian

'The characters are beautifully developed . . . recorded with such humour and sensitivity that it is an engrossing, sometimes laugh-out-loud story' *Write Away*

Also published by Macmillan Children's Books

Straw into Gold: Fairy Tales Re-Spun
(Previously published in hardback as
Hilary McKay's Fairy Tales)

The Skylarks' War

The Exiles trilogy

The Exiles

The Exiles at Home

Exiles in Love

HILARY MCKAY

The Exiles
At Home

MACMILLAN CHILDREN'S BOOKS

First published 1993 by Victor Gollancz Ltd.
This edition published 2019 by Macmillan Children's Books
an imprint of Pan Macmillan
20 New Wharf Road, London N1 9RR
Associated companies throughout the world
www.panmacmillan.com

ISBN 978-1-5290-1158-6

1 3 5 7 9 8 6 4 2

A CIP catalogue record for this book is available from the British Library.

Typeset by Jouve (UK), Milton Keynes
Printed and bound by CPI Group (UK) Ltd, Croydon CR0 4YY

For my mother

A Note From The Author

A long time ago, in a different world (no internet, no mobile phones) my mother sponsored the education of a young boy in Africa. His name was Joseck. Really, of course, the money went to his school, not the individual, and benefitted all the children there. However, the letters that were sent from home went directly to Joseck, and he sent his own letters back.

They opened up a way of life to us in quiet Lincolnshire that we had hardly considered. We lived in a much less outward-looking world in those pre-internet days.

Much later, when my own children were small, we sponsored more young people. Once again the letters came and went.

There was something about those letters – they brought their writers to life so well. They often had small drawings in the corners: a squirrel, a bus, some goats on a roof, a face. Sometimes on the thin paper we could detect a faint red smudge of African dust. They often seemed to fizz, with a sort of exuberant joy. I used them when I wrote *The Exiles at Home*.

That was more than twenty-five years ago. Many things

have changed and the home life of my characters was a different world. It was a time when children took themselves to school and back with no adult in charge. There was much less fuss, much less traffic on the roads, and consequently, much more freedom.

There was also much less understanding. Enormous gulfs between Joseck's world and ours. In those days we learnt about other countries in school, with atlases and Geography lessons – there was very little on TV. Every now and then *Blue Peter* would whisk us away for a while, or something would be reported on the news, but real life, the ordinary everyday life of people in another country was beyond our knowledge. No one I knew had been further than France – there was no internet and no instant messaging. We wrote letters, and waited slow weeks for replies. No wonder they meant so much to us.

In this new publication of *The Exiles at Home*, I have been able to smooth out some attitudes that would jar with new readers today. But the story is just the same. Ruth, Naomi, Rachel and Phoebe work as hard as they can (not always in the most sensible ways) for something they believe worth doing – helping out a friend.

Hilary McKay
March 2019

CHAPTER ONE

Ruth Conroy was thirteen and she was the eldest, which was sometimes difficult, with Naomi, Rachel and Phoebe, pushing from behind. If Ruth could have had one wish it would have been for adventures. Adventures in far-away countries, with exotic animals, and mountains and forests and white towns and red roads and blue seas and ice fields and bright colours and interesting people with stories to tell. Ruth had never been out of England, but she knew about these places because she had read too many books.

Next in the family was twelve-year old Naomi. Naomi lived one step back from real life, like a cat. Like a cat, she had many interesting thoughts, which she mostly did nothing about and kept in her head.

After Naomi came Rachel. Her life was mostly spent in the hard work of looking after Rachel. She did it as well as she possibly could, because somebody had to do it. If any of the Conroy girls were pretty, it was Rachel, not that anyone admitted it. Their father said they were all beautiful, and their mother said it wasn't how you looked, but how you behaved, that mattered. Rachel knew they were both wrong, but it was no use saying it, because nobody ever listened.

Last of all, came Phoebe, who was six years old and did as she liked, as well as anyone could with three bossy big sisters in a very small house.

The Conroy girls went to unspectacular schools where they didn't work hard, although they always regretted this when it came to school reports at the end of term.

The Christmas holidays began with the bringing home of school reports. Although these had been handed out in sealed envelopes with instructions to deliver them unopened, only Phoebe's arrived home this way. Phoebe was so serenely detached from other people's opinions of herself that the report on her term's work held no temptation at all. When her mother read aloud: 'Phoebe continues stubbornly to ignore all help and advice . . .' she glanced briefly up from the letter she was writing and remarked, 'Miss always says that,' before continuing unruffled with her message to Father Christmas. For several weeks now, a great deal of Phoebe's time had been spent this way.

Outdoors was rainy, but the Conroy family were lucky enough to have a real fire in their living room. Rachel was still in her school coat, enjoying the way the steam rose from her sleeves when she held them close to the heat. She had been watching as her sister wrote.

'You should post it up the chimney,' she said, as Phoebe began to add the usual row of kisses to the bottom of the page, but Phoebe preferred to leave her letters lying about where they could be discovered by her relations.

'What about your report, Rachel?' asked Mrs Conroy.

Rachel fumbled in her mitten for a while and then handed her mother a wet bundle of grey paper. She had dropped her envelope in a puddle on the way home from school in the hope of unsticking it. It had not only unstuck, it had disintegrated, the ink had run, and during its journey home squashed in the end of Rachel's mitten, it had fallen to pieces. All that it was possible to read were the two words, 'Rachel tries . . .' Rachel brightened up tremendously at these words, so much more encouraging than she had dared to hope.

'It could be short for "Rachel tries but fails",' Naomi pointed out.

'Yes,' agreed Ruth, 'or, "Rachel tries to do nothing," or "Rachel tries to drive me mad"!'

'You're just jealous,' said Rachel, 'because I've got a good report and you haven't.'

'No one ever gets good reports at our school,' replied Ruth. 'Mine was one of the best in the class, actually. We all opened them and looked.'

'Yours is disgraceful,' said her mother and read aloud, ' "Ruth's work suffers from an almost total lack of planning. Her homework is rarely completed on time and she appears spend a great deal of the school day in a dream!" '

'What's wrong with being in a dream?' asked Ruth. 'It's a survival technique. Anyway, mine's better than Naomi's. Hers doesn't even make sense!'

Naomi's report had puzzled everyone. It said that Naomi was one of the worst-motivated boys in the class and made no real attempt at any subject except football. Mrs Conroy read it again and passed it to Big Grandma, who had arrived that day to spend Christmas with the family.

'Frightful handwriting,' commented Big Grandma cheerfully, who had once been a teacher herself. 'Still, you must remember that it was probably written at dead of night by an exhausted, underpaid teacher, almost certainly driven mad by lack of sleep . . .'

'So you don't think we ought to complain?' asked Mrs Conroy.

'No!' cried Ruth, Naomi, Rachel, Phoebe and Big Grandma added, 'Perish the thought!'

'Christmas is no time for complaining,' agreed the children's father, who had been listening in silence to the chatter. 'Hey! Not there, Rachel!'

He was too late. Rachel, gathering together the fragments of her report, had wandered across the room searching for the magic words 'Rachel tries', and, having found them, sat down to gloat. She sat on the Christmas cake, newly iced and left to dry on the coffee table. Father Christmas, twelve reindeer, the North Pole and Rachel all sank together into a sudden valley of marzipan.

'I'm not eating that now!' remarked Phoebe, as Rachel ran wailing from the room, shedding tears and lumps of icing. A huge clean-up operation followed, during which Mrs Conroy forgot all about school reports. Ruth and Naomi took the cake away and resourcefully re-iced it.

'Even better than before,' said Ruth, and it was: a beautifully hilly landscape with Father Christmas and the reindeer now on cardboard skis. They sailed down the hillside beside a blue icing stream with chocolate button boulders.

'Reminds me of home,' said Big Grandma when she saw it. Home for Big Grandma was Cumbria, hills and streams and sheep. The girls had spent the summer there and Phoebe, remembering the sheep, rinsed three plastic lambs from her farmyard and stuck them into the icing snow.

'Phoebe! They look grey!' exclaimed her mother.

'Sheep do look grey against the snow,' said Big Grandma. 'We have lambs in the village already. And snow on the tops of the hills.'

Naomi, thinking of the six weeks spent in the Cumbrian hills, felt suddenly homesick for them. Climbing on to the windowsill she drew the curtains behind her, shutting out the bright, noisy room. The garden was grey and full of deep shadows.

'Snow!' begged Naomi silently to the dark sky, and leaning her forehead against the cold window-pane, she peered hopefully into the garden.

Ruth slid round the curtains, guessed immediately what Naomi was wishing for, and asked, 'Do you think it might?'

'It's all I really want for Christmas,' Naomi replied. 'I don't know why it never does. It always snows in books!'

5

'Look! There's Broken Beak,' said Ruth, as the tame family blackbird hopped out from under the hedge.

'He should be in bed. A cat might get him.'

Broken Beak looked enquiringly at the house and then up at the sky.

'He's waiting for something,' said Ruth.

She and Naomi gazed at the dark bundle of feathers, motionless upon the lawn. Magically, as they watched, a white star appeared on his black velvet back, and then slowly, in ones and twos, more snowflakes drifted down to balance on the blades of grass. Broken Beak gave a satisfied flounce of his feathers and disappeared back under the hedge.

'It worked!' exclaimed Naomi in delight. 'That's the first time ever I've wished a wish and it's really come true!'

'I wished it too. Is it going to stick?'

'It looks like it might. It's not melting anyway.'

'Don't tell the others yet, in case . . .'

'No.'

'Do you think Mum's forgotten about my report?' Naomi said, after a pause.

'Ages ago. Why? Are you glad your teacher mixed them up? Do you think it would have been awful?'

'I think,' said Naomi cautiously, 'that Mum might not have understood what the teacher was trying to say, even if she did get the right one. You know, they always have to write uncomplimentary things in case we get big-headed, but they never mean them. So they never *could* write what Mum wants to read, things like: "Naomi has worked very hard and done extremely well and is always polite and helpful".'

'No, they'd never write that,' agreed Ruth, 'because it simply isn't true! They . . .'

'Anyway,' Naomi interrupted hurriedly, 'the snow's settling! That's all that really matters!'

In the morning the ceilings were luminous with snow-light. Naomi and Ruth, who were sleeping on camp-beds in the living room so that Big Grandma could have their bedroom, rolled out at dawn to look at the garden. There they saw Phoebe, in her dressing-gown and slippers, marching solemnly across the lawn, admiring every footprint. Rachel was following her, stepping carefully into her sister's tracks so as not to spoil the snow. In places it came up to their knees.

Ruth and Naomi watched as their little sisters bent and scooped handfuls of snow into snowballs and then stowed the snowballs in their dressing-gown pockets. 'Hmm,' said Ruth thoughtfully, and slid her bed across the room to barricade the door.

'Just for ten minutes,' she said, 'until the snowballs melt or someone catches them.'

They waited until they heard giggling in the hall and saw the door handle turning slowly. After that, there was much heavy breathing and pushing on the door, whispered orders from Phoebe and then retreating footsteps and the sound of the fridge door being opened.

*

At breakfast time – which was late, with no bacon, because of the melted snowball floods in the fridge – Rachel suddenly announced, 'All I want for Christmas is a sledge!'

It was the first time she had been able to think of a present, although for weeks her parents had been asking, 'Isn't there anything you really want, Rachel?'

'Oh yes,' Rachel had replied, 'a real farm and a boat. Cows and sheep and horses and donkeys. One of those hot-air balloons!' She had never thought of anything reasonable; until now, on Christmas Eve, with the roads deep in snow and more to come by the look of the sky, she had suddenly announced, 'All I want is a sledge!'

'Sorry, Rachel,' said her mother, 'no shopping on Christmas Eve. Not that I can think of anywhere we could find a sledge.'

'What about Father Christmas?' Rachel asked.

'Father Christmas,' said Phoebe, 'isn't true. Everyone knows.'

'I should not care to say that,' Big Grandma remarked. 'Certainly tempting fate, on the twenty-fourth of December, to make rash remarks about the validity of Father Christmas!'

'Reckless,' agreed Mr Conroy solemnly.

'At school,' argued Phoebe, 'everyone knows it's just made up for children. And Rachel's older than me! She's nearly nine!'

'And you are not yet seven and I am seventy-one,' remarked Big Grandma, 'so who is right?'

'I only said what they say at school. Not what I think.'

'What do you think?' asked Mr Conroy.

'Thousands of things,' replied Phoebe.

That day the snow muffled all sounds. It slowed the speed of cars and walkers so that they were soft and heavy, like movements in a dream. It drew, with its whiteness, a clean blank page over the usual scribble of their lives.

'Everything seems more real than usual,' said Phoebe, but could not explain what she meant.

Martin-the-boy-next-door collected the girls to build a fort and dig paths, and his dog, huge golden Josh, chased snowballs down the street and snapped at falling snowflakes. Ruth waited until he wasn't looking and then buried herself in the drift under the beech hedge but Josh, in seconds, sniffed her out and snuffled and pawed the snow away.

'Josh, I love you,' said Ruth as his hairy, anxious face peered down at her.

'Josh is my favourite person,' remarked Rachel.

Martin, who was often called Martin-the-good, felt suddenly Christmassy and said, 'You can share him if you like. You can come round and borrow him.'

'Forever, or just for the snow?' asked Rachel, believing more and more in Christmas magic.

Christmas morning came, and Rachel got her sledge.

'Who did it come from?' asked Phoebe in disbelief, as Rachel stripped the wrappings away.

'Father Christmas,' said Rachel triumphantly.

'You see!' said her father.

Naomi heard Big Grandma ask her mother the same question and the whispered reply: 'John. All yesterday afternoon and half the evening with the wood he bought to make the new gate.'

'Ah! I noticed he kept disappearing.'

'He was out in the shed! I thought he'd freeze. He dried the varnish with my hairdryer at one o'clock in the morning . . . Oh, Naomi!'

'It's all right,' said Naomi. 'I didn't think it was Father Christmas.'

Phoebe, who had kept a copy of her letter-that-should-have-gone-up-the-chimney sat under the Christmas tree methodically unwrapping and ticking things off. Rachel loaded her sledge with all her unopened presents and started tugging it across the room.

'Oi! You're running me over!' said Ruth.

'Aren't you going to see what they are?' asked Mrs Conroy.

'Oh yes,' said Rachel, and sitting down on her sledge, unwrapped them all saying, 'Oh yes books, oh yes socks, oh yes a new bear . . .'

'He's got a zip in his back for pyjamas.'

'Oh yes,' said Rachel, not bothering to look. 'Oh yes, chocolates!'

'Look in the envelope!'

'Oh yes, money as well! And a school thing . . .'

'It's not a school thing, it's a Spirograph. It draws lovely . . .'

'Oh yes,' said Rachel and dumped all her presents back on her sledge and started pulling it across the room again.

After unwrapping some clothes, a few books and some chocolates from Big Grandma (with ten pound notes attached) Ruth and Naomi gloomily watched Rachel and Phoebe as they were gradually submerged in an ocean of wrapping paper, until Phoebe, glancing out of the window, exclaimed, 'Someone's been mucking up our snow!' Then they rushed outside and followed huge black sooty footprints to the garden shed and found two new bikes labelled 'Ruth' and 'Naomi', one red, one green, shiny beyond their wildest dreams, and with tinsel round the handlebars.

'Don't think we've ever had a better turkey,' Mr Conroy remarked at dinner-time.

'Free range,' said Big Grandma. 'Makes all the difference!'

'What do you mean?' asked Rachel.

'They wander round free,' explained Mr Conroy, 'they lead more natural lives!'

Phoebe, who had eaten an enormous dinner, despite having consumed chocolates all morning, stared in horror at the turkey.

'That turkey,' she announced, 'is dead! Dead!' she repeated. 'A dead animal.'

'Is it?' asked Rachel.

'Yes, and that's its corpse!'

'Phoebe, really!' said her mother, but Phoebe could not be stopped.

'Corpse!' she continued. 'I've eaten dead corpse!' and she

11

rushed off to the bathroom. When she emerged, pale and clammy, she announced, 'I'm a vegetarian!'

The snow stayed until almost the end of the holidays, prolonging the atmosphere of Christmas. With each fresh day of sunlight and snow showers and each night of frost and stars, the feeling of other-worldness increased.

'This is the best Christmas ever,' declared Rachel, who had been out from dawn to dusk, pulling a cargo of snowballs up and down the street. 'How long do you think the snow will last?'

'We've had snow in May before now,' said Mr Conroy.

'Heaven forbid!' exclaimed Big Grandma. 'I'm driving back to Cumbria tomorrow! Anyway, the temperature's been rising all day and the weather forecast said rain for tonight.'

The forecast proved to be correct. By morning the snow had gone, washed away by a combination of rain and Rachel's tears. Big Grandma recruited her granddaughters to help with her packing.

'Stay a bit longer,' Ruth urged. 'Stay till spring!'

'Imagine how your poor mother would feel, if I did,' replied Big Grandma. 'Come and sit on this suitcase lid!'

'She likes having you! We all do.'

'Bounce!' ordered Big Grandma. 'That's right. Now the other side. Where's Naomi?'

'She's checking that your oil and tyres and lights are all right.'

'Does she know how? Perhaps we'd better go down and

supervise. Ruth, you can carry that, and that, and that, and those, and hook a finger round this little bag and check under the bed before you come.'

'Do you have to go?' Naomi, very oily and windswept, met Big Grandma in the hall. 'Martin says the oil's all right, and three of your tyres and one of your lights.'

'Which one?'

'The outside one.'

'Good enough for me,' said Big Grandma cheerfully, 'I'll be home before dark. Cheer up, Naomi, you can have your room back! No more squirming on a camp-bed, being moulted on by the Christmas tree. Not that your bed is much more comfortable; it's got a terrible sag!'

'You could sleep in Ruth's for a change,' suggested Naomi.

'It's got loose legs,' said Ruth, staggering up under a load of Big Grandma's possessions, 'but you can have it if you like. The legs only come off if you turn over quickly.'

'No thank you,' said Big Grandma. 'At my age such novelties lose all their charm! It seems very quiet this morning. Where are Rachel and Phoebe?'

Rachel was lying on the back seat of Big Grandma's car, being dismal. 'Everything nice is ending,' she complained to Phoebe. 'First it was the end of Christmas Eve, then Christmas Day and Boxing Day, then the end of the turkey and the Christmas cake, then the end of last year. And now it's the end of the snow and Big Grandma and tonight it will be the end of the holidays!' She frowned at her feet, resting on the inside roof of the car among a pattern of small black footprints. 'Look, my trainers are all worn out! Nobody cares!'

'I wish I had the keys,' said Phoebe, sitting in the driver's seat. 'Naomi never checked the horn. I'll be legal to drive in only ten years,' and she pushed in the clutch and put the car in gear. 'First, second, third, fourth, reverse. All I need are the keys!'

'Big Grandma says you have to help pack!' Naomi arrived and dumped a cardboard box full of books on Rachel's stomach. 'So you can open the car door when you see me coming with more stuff.'

'Get that box off me, then,' said Rachel.

'Ask Phoebe,' said Naomi, and dashed back through the gusty rain into the house.

'It's going to be hard getting your Christmas lawnmower in,' Ruth said to Big Grandma. 'Shall I take the tinsel off it?'

'Certainly not, I like it very much. Help Naomi carry it out!'

'Phoebe!' croaked Rachel from the back seat, under her box of books. 'I'm suffocating! I've fainted. I can feel my head going black!'

'Here come Ruth and Naomi with the lawn-mower,' remarked Phoebe, climbing out to open the boot.

'Mind the tinsel,' ordered Naomi, 'Big Grandma wants to keep it. Look at your disgusting trainers, Rachel! You've piggled holes in both of them and you've paddled mud all over the roof!'

'I didn't piggle!' said Rachel indignantly, unfainting for a moment. 'They wore! Get this box off me!'

'Phoebe will. We're busy!' said Naomi, and headed back to the house where Ruth was complaining to Big Grandma. 'I wish I was going with you. There's nothing to do here.'

'You must think positively,' said Big Grandma. 'You girls have too easy a life, that's your trouble! You've got bicycles and legs and brains, you ought to be able to entertain yourselves! You're an unenterprising pair!'

'You know it's boring here!'

'I haven't been bored,' said Big Grandma. 'Put those two bags in the car, Ruth.'

'How do you tell broken ribs?' asked Ruth, on returning.

'Tickle them,' said Big Grandma. 'Don't forget my wellingtons, Naomi.'

Ruth and Naomi together removed the box from Rachel's stomach and tickled her broken ribs. Rachel screamed, but sat up quickly.

'Told you they weren't broken,' said Naomi.

'How do you know?' demanded Rachel.

'You'd be writhing in agony by now if they were.'

Rachel writhed a bit, hoping to make her sisters feel guilty, but they had all disappeared indoors. She followed them and writhed again in front of Big Grandma.

'Do you itch somewhere?' asked Big Grandma.

'It's my broken ribs,' Rachel told her crossly, as they all trooped outside.

'Must be painful,' said Big Grandma. 'I'd better be off.' She kissed Mrs Conroy. 'Say goodbye to John for me, and don't stand out here in the rain. Goodbye, girls! Be astonishing and good and brave. It's been lovely; I'll ring when I'm home.'

She tooted her horn, and was gone.

Damp and disconsolate, they trailed back into the house.

'I don't feel like going back to the ordinary world,' grumbled Ruth.

'What ordinary world?' asked Phoebe.

CHAPTER TWO

School began the next morning and the Conroy house filled with chaos.

'You have had weeks,' complained Mrs Conroy to Naomi, 'to pack your school bags and put PE kits to be washed, never mind homework . . . did you have homework? Now . . .'

There was an enormous crash, followed by screams and tears, the sound of them shaking the whole house. Mrs Conroy groaned and ran; Ruth came in from the garden, listened briefly, said, 'Oh,' and began grating cheese for Broken Beak the blackbird; Phoebe looked up from her cereal and murmured, 'Rachel.'

'Fallen down the loo *again*,' agreed Naomi, as the yells became more and more deafening. 'Who put the butter right under my elbow? What gets butter off?'

'Tar,' answered Ruth, adding chopped raisins to the cheese, 'or is it butter gets tar off? I don't know. Do you think I've got enough food here to last him all day?'

Naomi and Phoebe looked at the heap, considering.

'There's still a few dried-up mince pies he could have,' said Naomi, 'if Rachel hasn't . . . gosh, listen to her!'

'*All right, Rachel*!' they heard their mother shout. 'You *won't* fall down the hole!'

'Get me out! Get me out!' Rachel continued to howl.

'Do you think she *could* go down the hole?' asked Phoebe. 'Or not?'

'Not,' said Ruth.

'Oh,' said Phoebe, sounding very disappointed.

Naomi scribbled a last random answer to her holiday homework. Ruth dashed into the garden to take Broken Beak his supplies and to shout to Martin-next-door, who was outside with Josh, 'Martin! Make the bus wait for me and Naomi if we're late.'

Martin nodded, looked towards the house, grinned and asked, 'Rachel again? I heard a lot of squealing.'

'She'll be out now, Mum went up to her,' said Ruth, and rushed back in.

By standing on the lavatory and leaning carefully out of the bathroom window it was possible to see right along the road to the bus stop before theirs. It was Ruth and Naomi's school-bus-early-warning system. They could do this quite easily, but Rachel had to stand on tiptoe and she never remembered to close the lid.

'You Big Ones shouldn't make her to do it,' Mrs Conroy said crossly, down in the kitchen with Rachel in fresh socks. 'It ruins her slippers and she might hurt herself! Not to mention the bathroom floor!'

'They didn't make me,' said Rachel, 'Naomi's paying me. I'm saving up.'

'What for?'

'Things for my sledge,' said Rachel vaguely.

'You're a disgrace,' Mrs Conroy said. 'You all are. And you're going to be late again. Look at the time and none of you ready!'

'I am.' Phoebe remarked. She wore Rachel's gloves and Naomi's scarf and in her school bag was Ruth's packed lunch. She dodged behind her mother when her sisters all pounced to ransack her.

'The bus!' ordered Mrs Conroy, pushing them out of the way. 'Ruth, Naomi! Run!'

They ran, out the house and along the street, racing towards the bus stop where Martin-the-good stood with one foot on the kerb and the other on the bus, very much annoying the driver, but doing as Ruth had asked.

'I can't manage this every morning,' he grumbled, when the girls finally arrived. 'It's a really stressful way to start the day!'

'We know. You are good. Tomorrow we'll do it for you.'

'You never will.'

'One day anyway . . .'

'I bet.'

'You are . . .'

'You don't have to keep saying it.'

'Good.'

Martin sighed. He couldn't help it. He had no choice. He was good.

The school bus gathered speed and overtook Rachel and Phoebe as, at snail's pace, they plodded along the road to their primary school with their mother. Rachel and Phoebe waved excitedly. Ruth and Naomi pretended not to see them. Martin, who was kind as well as good, waved back.

All along the bus, people were seated in pairs, copying each other's homework. In the back seat, Egg-Yolk Wendy, the Charity Monitor, sat eating Gavin's packed lunch.

'Gavin's my new boyfriend,' she called along the aisle to Ruth. 'I got him at the weekend!'

Gavin stared at his knees in shame. Wendy unwrapped his chocolate biscuit and bit it in half.

'Gavin, you idiot!' said Martin. 'Why'd you let her?'

'I didn't want it anyway,' mumbled Gavin, referring to his biscuit.

Ruth, sitting next to Naomi, gazed out of the window and felt strange. Sort of floaty and light and unencumbered. It was such an unusual feeling for a grey January day, that she could not understand it and wondered why. They were half-way to school before she realised.

'I've forgotten my school bags,' she announced, suddenly panic-stricken, 'and my PE kit! Let me off! Let me off!' she shouted to the driver.

The bus screeched to a halt.

'Somebody sick?' called the driver, 'If so, get out!'

'It's no good stopping,' Naomi told him. 'It's too late now!'

'Good Lord in heaven,' said the driver. 'If I have to clean this bus again. What a way to earn a living!'

'And I'd even done my homework,' Ruth said sadly, 'no one will ever believe me!'

Martin realized that the driver thought Ruth had been sick, and kindly wobbled up to the front of the bus to explain.

Wendy, seeing that the journey was going to take longer than usual, thought she might as well eat Gavin's apple but she said, 'Do you like apples, Gav?' before she bit into it.

'Not much,' said Gavin, too late to say anything else.

The driver wondered about asking for a transfer.

'How am I going to get through the day?' Ruth asked Naomi as they arrived at school. 'Why are you staring like that?'

Naomi, looking at the sister properly for the first time that morning, demanded, 'What are you wearing?'

'What do you mean?'

'Look what you're wearing!'

Ruth looked down and there, tucked neatly into her school skirt, was her pyjama top. There was nothing underneath it, and no tie or jumper on top to disguise it.

'Didn't you wash this morning?' asked Naomi, slightly shocked.

'Of course I did! I must have put it back on again! Why didn't you notice before? Why didn't Mum? Why didn't Martin, even? Why didn't *anyone*?'

'Why didn't *you*?' asked Naomi. 'Pink with teddy bears! You couldn't have chosen worse!'

'I didn't choose.'

'Well, you'll just have to button up your blazer and wrap your scarf round tight,' said Naomi.

This Ruth did, and it worked fairly well until PE, when there was no way of hiding the pink teddy bears any longer. With no PE kit she couldn't go outside to play hockey with the rest. Instead, she was sent to the library, a dim, chilly room, with a borrowed pen and scrap paper, and instructions to make a list of all she had forgotten that day and would remember the next. It was a long list, but not as long as a double PE lesson. Ruth looked around for something to do and decided that it was so cold, she'd collect all the books on Africa. She took them away to a dark corner beside the newspapers and tried to warm herself up by reading them. She spent all afternoon there and went home shivering. Mrs Conroy looked at her very suspiciously and put her to bed.

'They've got it next door, too,' she said. 'Mrs Collingwood was telling me. The baby went down with it yesterday. Martin's had it so she's hoping for the best!'

'Had what?' asked Ruth.

'Doesn't mean a thing, I told her,' continued Mrs Conroy. 'They catch it twice, as often as not. You'll perhaps feel better when the spots come out!'

'What spots?' demanded Ruth.

'Hanging round there all Christmas, borrowing that dog is

what's done it,' said Mrs Conroy. 'I must get downstairs; I've left cakes in the oven.'

'Asking for what?' Ruth called after her departing mother.

'Trouble!' Mrs Conroy called back to her. 'Lie down and go to sleep!'

It was Ruth's third chicken-pox day; she was white with red dots. Her mother, saying she was less trouble in bed than out, was holding her captive in her bedroom. It was very lonely and she was glad when Naomi came in.

'Mum's been going on about our bedroom being a mess,' Naomi remarked. 'She sent me up to look at it.'

'It's only a mess in patches,' said Ruth. 'Bits of it are still tidy. I'm glad you came up. I wanted to ask you to do something for me.'

'I'm too busy.'

'You don't know what it is yet!'

'Much too busy to do anything,' said Naomi firmly, 'especially if I've got to clear all this up by myself!'

'It won't take any time, hardly. And this room doesn't need clearing up, there's still lots of tidy patches.'

'Mum says I'm not allowed to upset you because of your temperature, so perhaps I'd better leave the mess anyway.'

I am upset already, Ruth thought, and aloud she asked, 'Naomi, will you get the post for me? I'm scared something might come for me and Mum or Dad'll get it first.'

'Why?' asked Naomi. 'What have you done?'

'Only written a letter, but I don't want Mum or Dad to

23

know. Couldn't you grab the postman and get anything that comes for me?'

'Funny I never noticed before,' said Naomi, still gazing at the ceiling.

'Noticed what?'

'How tidy is it?'

'Will you get the post for me, then? You're not listening!'

'I am. Tell me what the letter's about. Is it about something disgusting, like those bones you collected last summer? Is that why Mum and Dad can't know? When did you send it, anyway?'

'That awful first day at school, when I had to go to the library instead of PE. It was freezing cold, so I got out all the books on Africa to see if reading them would warm me up. And I looked at the newspapers from last year, and in that one that Big Grandma has, there was an advert.' Ruth watched Naomi's face out of the corner of her eye. 'It said that for only ten pounds a month you can sponsor someone in Africa to go to school, and they write to you and you write back to them . . .'

'I'd pay ten pounds a month not to go to school,' remarked Naomi.

'So I filled in the form,' continued Ruth, ignoring her, 'and sent off the money straight away.'

'You're nuts!' said Naomi, suddenly waking up. 'Anyway, what with?'

'A pen from the lost-property drawer.'

'I meant, what money?'

'Big Grandma's ten pounds,' said Ruth, sighing. 'You have

to send the first month's money and fill in a form to say you'll sponsor whoever it is for at least a year, and say that you're over eighteen.'

'Well, you're not!'

'I know. But I ticked the box to say I was.'

'So they're going to write to you, and you have to send off ten pounds every month? And you've started it already!' said Naomi, astonished.

'I don't think it's such a bad idea. Or it wouldn't be, if I had any money. But I can't tell Mum, she'd be furious about me saying I was eighteen. So would Dad. They'll say it isn't honest!'

'Well, it isn't,' said Naomi virtuously. 'Anyway, what do you want me to do?'

'Just get the post, that's all. Until I can get up again.'

'Oh, all right,' agreed Naomi, 'but it's all I'm doing to help!'

For the next few days Naomi watched the post for Ruth, hanging round the gate until the postman came, and then volunteering to take the letters inside.

Waiting for the post made Naomi even later than usual for the school bus every morning. The driver grumbled at Martin, who every morning heroically kept one foot on the kerb and the other on the bus. Wendy got very indignant and protested to Ruth that it made her late for everything. Even Gavin, the mildest of people, confided in a whisper to Martin that it gave his compulsory girlfriend more time than ever to eat his packed lunch. Martin passed on this complaint, together with several of his own, and Naomi in turn reported them all to Ruth, who was still confined in their bedroom, quite poorly but recovering slowly.

'Sorry,' said Ruth.

One morning the postman handed Naomi a very scruffy envelope addressed to 'R.N.R.P. Conroy'.

'Is that you?' he asked.

'Yes.'

'Boyfriend?'

'NO!'

'I can always tell,' he said, winking.

'You can't!' snapped Naomi, recognising one of the rare, welcome letters from Graham, their friend from the summer holidays at Big Grandma's house in Cumbria. Graham's letters, usually written at the kitchen table on his Cumbrian farm, were largely incomprehensible to the girls, but still treasured. They were full of descriptions of football matches, farm machinery and local weather conditions and always began, 'Mum says I ought to write . . .'

The postman told Naomi off, the next time she appeared with her hand held out.

'You can't expect the poor lad to write constantly,' he said severely. 'There's just one for your sister,' and he delivered the long-awaited brown envelope rather reprovingly. Naomi carried it in to Ruth between her fingertips, as if it might explode.

'I'm glad it's Saturday,' she said crossly. 'You can get the post yourself from now on! It's too embarrassing!'

'Don't you want to see what's in it?' asked Ruth, seeing that Naomi was preparing to leave again.

'I'm going into town,' replied Naomi. 'Anyway, I told you I didn't want anything to do with it, and I don't! Will Mum let you out today, do you think?'

'No she won't!' said Mrs Conroy, appearing suddenly in the doorway. 'Don't stuff things under your jumper, Ruth! You'll make it go all baggy! No, Ruth isn't going anywhere today; she can have a quiet weekend before school on Monday. And you two leave Rachel and Phoebe alone. I don't want them vanishing. I've told them they're not moving one step from my sight until their bedroom carpet is clear!'

Ruth and Naomi peered curiously round their little sisters' bedroom door. Rachel and Phoebe were sitting sulkily on their bunk-beds, obviously appalled by the task in front of them. The entire bedroom floor, except for a narrow track leading to the bunks, was covered in toys, books, clothes and bits of paper.

'I can't find my Snoopy socks,' said Phoebe.

'I'm surprised you can find your feet in all that mess,' said Mrs Conroy crossly, 'and it's about time that sledge went down to the shed, waking us up every night! I must have the only daughter in England that takes a sledge to bed with her!'

'Does she take it to bed with her?' asked Naomi, surprised. 'Is that what the crashes are? I thought it was only Rachel falling out!'

'Yes,' said Phoebe, 'every night, and then when it falls out, she gets up and drags it back up again and treads all over my face. And what if it falls on my head, that's what I say.'

'Tie it to the bed,' suggested Naomi practically.

'Then when it falls off, it swings down and whacks Phoebe. I've tried that,' said Rachel.

'Everything to be put away before I come back up!' interrupted Mrs Conroy, closing the door on their squabbles. 'Or I'll do it myself and It Will All Go In The Bin!'

Ruth disappeared to lock herself in the bathroom, where she could read her letter in peace. Naomi, whose Christmas money had been weighing on her mind ever since she had received it, prepared to go in to town.

'Don't go wasting it all at once,' advised Mrs Conroy.

'I'm only going to look at things,' said Naomi, smoothing and admiring her ten pound note. She had no intention of spending it, but on that grey January Saturday, she rashly took out with her. And that was the end of it.

Some days later, she tried to explain to Ruth what had happened. 'Glue,' she remembered. 'I bought some glue. We never have any; ours is always dried up. And I bought some gold stars, like they used to stick on our books when we were little. Two packets. I took them to school.'

Ruth remembered the stars. Naomi had stuck them all over her books and subsequently spent a lunch-time detention peeling them off again.

'And some strawberries.'

'In January!'

'And a newspaper. To sit on while I ate them; the bench was wet. And a lamb chop and a packet of biscuits for a poor thin dog that was tied to a post.'

'That was nice.'

'And a football magazine, to try and find out what Graham is always talking about. But Martin's borrowed it; I'll get it back though, before we write to Cumbria again. And some stamps. And some dog treats for teaching Josh tricks, but Rachel's been eating them.'

'That must have been nearly all your money gone, then,' said Ruth.

'Yes,' said Naomi, 'that was nearly all of it. It went fast.'

'What a waste!'

'Well, look what you did with yours!' exclaimed Naomi, 'and you've said you'll pay ten pounds a month! What are you going to do? You only get a pound a week pocket money, so even if you don't spend a penny of it, you'll be minus six pounds a month!'

'I was wondering if you might like to share with me.'

'Share my pocket money? No thank you!'

'Well, you could just look at the stuff they sent.' Ruth pulled her envelope out from under her mattress. 'I've even got a photograph of him. He's ten and he's called Joseck.'

'Joseck?' asked Naomi, peering over Ruth's shoulder to look at the picture of a smiling boy in school uniform. 'He looks very brainy. That must be his school behind.'

'I looked up where they live in my atlas,' said Ruth. 'Do you want to see?'

'In a minute,' Naomi was still studying the photograph. 'What are you going to do? You can't tell someone you'll sponsor them, then just let them down.'

'I'm not going to!' said Ruth, indignantly.

'When do you need the next ten pounds for?'

'February,' replied Ruth, and they both stared thoughtfully out of the window.

'Ten pounds by February,' said Naomi. 'That's not long. It's not even two whole weeks.'

'I know.'

'Got anything saved up?'

'Not enough. Not even half enough.'

'Well,' said Naomi, eventually. 'I suppose we'd better go and see what Rachel and Phoebe have done with their Christmas money.'

Rachel and Phoebe were out spending the afternoon in the garden, being taught to groom Josh under Martin's supervision. Josh had been brushed and brushed until he shone and handfuls of his red-gold fur were floating all over the garden.

'You'll brush him bare,' remarked Naomi. 'He looks thinner already.'

'We've cleaned his teeth,' said Rachel, 'with dog toothpaste. It's peppermint, like people's!'

'Did you eat it?'

'Only a bit.'

'I've always wanted a horse,' said Phoebe, dreamily combing the feathers on Josh's front legs.

'Yes, but he's a dog,' pointed out Martin.

'I know, but I call him a horse in my head,' answered Phoebe, who could always ignore reality when she needed to.

Naomi gave Rachel and Josh one each of her dog treats. They both sat up and begged.

'It's nice for Josh not to be the only one who has to beg,'

said Ruth, watching them. 'He must feel a fool doing it on his own.'

'More likely feels a fool doing it with Rachel,' answered Martin.

Phoebe took two of the dog treats and tried to make Rachel and Josh balance them on their noses, but they both jerked their heads and ate them at once.

'Can I have two more?' asked Phoebe.

'You should buy some yourself,' said Naomi, 'you've got all that money that Big Grandma gave you.'

'Yes, but I put it in my train,' explained Phoebe, 'before I thought.'

Ruth and Naomi sighed with frustration. Phoebe's train, given to her by Big Grandma as a christening present, was very old and, Mrs Conroy said, quite valuable. Its enormous disadvantage was that although it had a slot to put your money in, there was no way of getting it back out again. Careful shaking sometimes allowed the reckless saver to extract coins from its insides, but paper money would be different. It was already full of scraps of paper anyway; Phoebe had a habit of writing important messages to herself and stuffing them in her train. It had occurred to no one that she might push her Christmas money into it as well.

'Anyway, it's safe there,' said Phoebe comfortably. 'Rachel's lost hers!'

Ruth looked at Naomi in despair. Never, it seemed, could forty pounds have been disposed of with so little to show for it.

'I haven't lost it,' said Rachel, 'I've put it in a secret place.'

'In the house?'

'No.'

'In the garden?'

'No.'

'Not at school somewhere?'

'Course not.'

'Are Mum and Dad looking after it for you, then?'

'No.'

'Sounds like you've lost it,' said Naomi.

'Why d'you want to know?' Rachel asked suspiciously.

'I don't,' said Naomi. 'I was just thinking about money. I was wondering how people got it.'

'They go to work and earn it,' said Martin. 'My dad says the only money worth having is money you've earned yourself!'

'You can sell things,' said Phoebe, 'like I will sell you my train for a thousand pounds. Nine-hundred-and-ninety pounds profit for me!'

'The best way,' said Rachel, scrabbling through a flower bed as she spoke, 'is to find treasure. Buried treasure. Lumps of gold and rings and diamonds. I've found something already! What is it?'

'A tulip bulb,' said Ruth, taking it off her and inspecting it. 'Put it back!'

'Treasure,' repeated Rachel dreamily. 'People do. Look how I found that bulb without even trying! Gold and diamonds and stuff must be all over the place! Jewellers' shops are full of it. Even Mum's got a bit. And what happens to all the old stuff nobody wants any more? It must be lying around somewhere!'

Everyone stared at Rachel. Obviously she had given the subject a great deal of thought.

'Old stuff gets melted down, I suppose,' said Martin practically.

'I've never heard of anyone melting it down!'

'Or put in museums.'

'I've been to a museum,' argued Rachel. 'It was full of china and old clothes and boring statues. Hardly any treasure. I looked.'

At that moment a diversion was created. Mrs Collingwood, Martin's mother, appeared round the corner of the house with a pushchair. In it, screaming, sat Martin's little brother.

'Martin, I'm going to have to leave Peter with you,' Mrs Collingwood announced, parking the pushchair beside them. 'Dad will be back very soon. Give him his tea and I expect he'll cheer up. Mrs Conroy says she's about if you need her, and perhaps the girls will help!'

Martin's mother was a solicitor; she was clever and practical, and assumed that everyone else was as well, except those unfortunate people who demanded from the police station that she come and rescue them. Rachel adored Martin's mother because she always called her 'My Little Pet'. Phoebe, however, more or less detested her because her name for Phoebe was 'Sausage'. Phoebe did not like to think of herself as anyone's sausage.

Now Mrs Collingwood bent down to Peter's teary, purple, dripping face and said, 'Be a good boy for Martin! Smile for Mummy! Smiley-smiley!' and as Peter's screwed-up features uncreased for a moment, exclaimed, 'That's my precious!', kissed him, and was gone.

However, she had hardly closed the garden gate before Peter hiccuped and took an enormous breath to start howling again. Ruth gazed thoughtfully at him. He was not what she called precious. Still a bit chicken-poxy, practically bald although he was nearly two, crimson, pudgy and equipped, Martin had told her, with very sharp teeth. Usually she would have kept as far away as possible, but now she had money to raise. And here was Peter, crying out (literally) for a babysitter.

Naomi, Rachel and Phoebe had disappeared with a suddenness that was not flattering to Peter. Even Josh had jumped over the garden wall and gone home.

'Do you need some help?' Ruth asked Martin, above the din that his little brother was making.

'What can you do?' asked Martin, not fainting with gratitude as Ruth had hoped he would. 'I agree you ought to do something, considering the number of times I've held up the bus for you, but what can you do?'

'I could probably stop him screaming,' said Ruth. 'Me and Naomi invented a way to stop Phoebe screaming when she was a baby. It nearly always worked.'

'Well, why doesn't everyone do it if it works? Peter's been screaming for nearly two years!'

'Not everyone is strong enough to do it,' replied Ruth, 'or they haven't got a long, straight place to run. We used to do it in the park. Is he strapped in tight?'

'Of course he is. He escapes otherwise.'

'Good,' said Ruth, wheeling Peter out of the gate and on to the path. 'Now you come along on the outside, by the kerb, just in case!'

'In case what?'

Ruth did not reply. Taking a deep breath, she gripped the pushchair handles and began to run, faster and faster, until the hedges went past in a blur and the ground looked like a grey river beneath her feet and they reached the end of the road and swung back round, and Martin no longer had breath to shout 'What are we doing?' and Peter, far from screaming, was roaring with laughter and slapping his fat knees. By the time they reached the garden gate again, there was not a trace of a tear on his face.

'See?' said Ruth complacently, when she got her breath back. 'It used to work just like that on Phoebe, only Mum could never do it because she couldn't run fast enough.'

'Good dog! Good dog!' shouted Peter, his only two words, whacking the sides of his chariot.

'Now what?' asked Martin.

'Well,' said Ruth, 'then it's the hard bit. You have to do it again only a bit slower, and then again, and then perhaps again until you get down to walking. After that you can stop, because they're usually exhausted.'

'*They're* exhausted!' interrupted Martin.

'You can push this time,' Ruth told him, and at the end of the second run, Peter was distinctly drooping. 'He can't be as tough as Phoebe was,' remarked Ruth, surveying him. 'Take him indoors and feed him quick, before he goes to sleep. You might even be able to get him to bed.'

Peter looked at Ruth. He could not tell her that he had been bored and frustrated and that she had been fast and exciting but nevertheless, he was grateful.

'Good dog,' he said approvingly.

'That means "thank you",' translated Martin. 'Thanks.'

'That's all right,' said Ruth, as Peter was escorted indoors. Possibly, she thought, she would become indispensable and could put her babysitting prices up and up. She might get rich. Perhaps Peter was precious, after all. Visions of herself as a next-door, very expensive, very exclusive Mary Poppins filled her mind.

'That worked quickly,' remarked Naomi as Ruth, rather pink-faced from running in the cold air, returned indoors. 'Phoebe didn't believe me when I told her we used to do that to her!'

'Mum wouldn't have let you,' said Phoebe, looking very mutinous.

'Mum wouldn't have let you what?' asked Mrs Conroy, opening the dining room door at that moment. 'Lay the table please, Ruth, and Naomi, pop and make the salad, will you? You two Little Ones, clear up all this mess!'

'Mum, you wouldn't have let them run me up and down in a pushchair to stop me screaming, would you? Anyway, I didn't scream!'

'Round and round the park they used to push you,' recalled Mrs Conroy smiling, 'I remember now!'

'What if I'd fallen out?' asked Phoebe, outraged.

'You were strapped in. Anyway, they didn't go all that fast. Ruth would only have been about eight. Come on, clear up all that paper!'

Phoebe had been converting the box her Christmas slippers arrived in into a cage. Cardboard bars were glued across the front, and now she stuck a notice across the top saying,

'BEWAR OF THE
RORIN PIGS'

Between the bars she slid the latest school photographs of Ruth and Naomi.

'I might easily have fallen out,' she said. 'And what if people had laughed?'

'Really, Phoebe,' exclaimed Mrs Conroy, although she could not help laughing herself. 'It was all a long time ago!'

'I don't care,' said Phoebe. 'I'm starting a zoo.' She fetched her bear from the bedroom and sat him outside the cage so that he could see Ruth and Naomi, the Roaring Pigs, in the zoo.

Tea-time was unusually quiet that day. Ruth, once again preoccupied by her urgent need for money, ignored all Phoebe's dark glances towards the zoo on the windowsill. Rachel was depressed by the thought that it was her turn to wash the dishes after tea. Partly to postpone this, she finished off all the bread and butter and took a third helping of salad.

'Can I have some of Phoebe's sardines?' she asked. 'I've run out of ham.'

'Is Phoebe eating sardines?' asked Naomi in surprise. 'I thought she was a vegetarian!'

'I am.' Phoebe, carefully shrouding a sardine in a lettuce leaf, looked up defensively.

'Sardines are animals,' argued Naomi.

'Leave Phoebe alone,' Mr Conroy interrupted. 'If she's happy eating sardines, let her enjoy them in peace!'

'They haven't got legs,' said Phoebe, but all the same she unwrapped her sardine and gazed at it uncertainly.

'They've got tails,' Naomi remarked.

'Enough of this conversation,' announced Mrs Conroy firmly. 'Rachel, you can start clearing the table. Ruth and Naomi will help you. Phoebe, finish your tea properly!'

'I can't,' said Phoebe, 'they *have* got tails!' She sat mutinously at the table with her father, while Mrs Conroy left to supervise the washing-up.

'Leave them if you like,' said her father. 'No one will mind.'

'I mind,' said Phoebe, crossly.

'Well, then, pass me your plate and I'll make you a sandwich,' said Mr Conroy. 'You can see if that helps.'

Phoebe handed over her plate and her father reassembled its contents into a more discreet form. 'There you are,' he said, 'what the eye doesn't see . . . Why have you stuck Ruth and Naomi in prison?'

'It's a zoo, not a prison.'

'Just as bad.'

'It was a case of offended dignity,' said Mrs Conroy, reappearing for a moment.

Phoebe, chewing her sandwich, left the table to poke a bit of lettuce through the bars to Ruth.

'What if I took her out?' asked Mr Conroy.

'She would still be in,' replied Phoebe, 'in my mind.'

'What did she do?'

'Said I screamed,' explained Phoebe with her mouth full, 'when I was a baby. Like Peter next door. I didn't, did I?'

'You were the soul of discretion,' said Mr Conroy solemnly.

'Did Ruth and Naomi scream?'

'Continually.'

Phoebe looked pleased and, swallowing the last of her sandwich, leaned companionably against her father as she admired her captives.

'You wouldn't put your poor old dad in a zoo, would you?' asked Mr Conroy, looking down at her.

'No,' said Phoebe.

In the kitchen, Rachel dumped plates into the washing-up bowl and pulled them out again straight away.

'I'm not drying that,' said Naomi, 'it's still got a whole sardine on it.'

'I'll wash if you like,' Ruth offered, 'for fifty pence.'

'Ten,' said Rachel.

'Forty.'

'Twenty.'

'Oh all right.'

'D'you need money that much?' asked Naomi, as Rachel vanished before Ruth could change her mind.

'You know I do. I'm going to see if I can baby-sit Peter, but I still need ten pounds now. I've got to send it off soon. I've only got three saved up. How much have you got?'

'Three,' said Naomi, 'and a bit of change from Big Grandma's ten pound note, about eighty pence.'

'That's seven then,' said Ruth, 'with Rachel's money. It's not enough.'

Beside the kitchen sink stood an old wooden clog, which the Conroys used to drop all the odds and ends in found lying round the kitchen. Ruth emptied its contents on to the table. There were several buttons and elastic bands, the three plastic lambs that had been on the Christmas cake, a scattering of coppers and a few five pence pieces, a tooth, half a packet of mustard and cress seed, and a diamond and sapphire ring.

'Good heavens!' said Mrs Conroy, coming in and picking it up. 'That's Mother's ring! I didn't even know she'd left it!'

'Please can I have the change?' asked Ruth.

'Yes, I suppose so,' agreed Mrs Conroy, turning over the contents of the clog. 'Rachel's tooth! I never know what to do with teeth! It seems a bit heartless to throw them away. Some mothers keep them, and first shoes and bits of hair and goodness knows what.'

'So what do you do with them?' asked Naomi.

'Well, throw them away, I'm afraid,' confessed Mrs Conroy. 'After all, there's four of you; it would end up as bad as Ruth's bone collection if I didn't. And I once caught Rachel recycling teeth, taking them off my dressing table and putting them back under her pillow. Your father paid out night after night without noticing! Thank you for washing up.'

'If we find any more bits of money lying about, can we keep it?' asked Naomi. 'It's for charity.'

'If you're that hard-up,' agreed Mrs Conroy, 'one good turn deserves another! Something's been rattling round the washing machine, if you want to unscrew the filter and have a look. And there's twenty pence in your father's shaving mug, and speaking of good turns, I've been meaning to mention. I'm going back to work this spring. You two Big Ones especially, are going to find yourselves helping out a bit more.'

'Back to nursing?' asked Ruth. 'Can you remember how?'

'There's a refresher course,' Mrs Conroy said. 'It will only be part-time when they need extra staff.'

Ruth, grovelling round the back of the washing machine, emerged with forty pence and a lot of fluff.

'I knew,' said Naomi unexpectedly. 'Big Grandma told me. She said we'd have to help with Rachel and Phoebe. Well, at least they're house-trained, not like Peter! There's ninety pence in this shoe.' She pushed the change over to Ruth.

'I hope it's for a good cause,' remarked Mrs Conroy, watching them. 'Yes, I always liked nursing, and Grandma tells me you managed very well last summer, looking after each other.'

'Did she?' asked Naomi, looking very surprised.

'You're growing up fast now,' continued Mrs Conroy,

ignoring Naomi on purpose. 'Time you had a bit more responsibility.'

Ruth and Naomi wondered what their mother would say if she knew how much responsibility they had recently undertaken. 'Seven pounds ninety, eight pounds thirty,' counted Ruth when Mrs Conroy had gone. 'Eight pounds fifty, nearly enough,' she added, when Naomi produced the shaving mug's twenty pence.

'We ought to try scooping down the backs of the living room chairs,' suggested Naomi. 'We haven't done it for ages. Big Grandma said it would be good for all of us.'

'Scooping down chairs?'

'Mum going to work.'

'Oh.'

The chairs produced a further fifty pence, numerous hair-slides and a quantity of nutshells.

'Nine pounds,' said Naomi, 'and that's the lot. We won't be able to do this again you know; all this must have been piling up for ages.'

Despite further searching, that really did seem to be the lot, and it had taken all evening to find. But Peter unexpectedly saved them in the morning.

'Naomi!' Mrs Collingwood stopped Naomi as she passed the house. 'My poor Peter owes you an apology, I'm afraid! Dreadfully sick all over your mag last night!' And she showed Naomi the damp and disgusting remains of her football magazine. Naomi stepped backwards hastily.

'You'll have to get yourself another!' said Mrs Collingwood.

'Can't say I'm sorry, because it might have been the carpet. Martin says two pounds will cover it, so there we are, and we're very sorry, aren't we, Peter-pet?'

Peter, who was squirming in his mother's arms, didn't look sorry. He hung his tongue out at Naomi, and then grabbed the magazine and stuffed it in his mouth.

'Chews everything!' remarked Mrs Collingwood cheerfully. 'Teeth! Wave bye-bye!'

Naomi, not quite sure who was being addressed, herself or Peter, waved bye-bye.

'Good old Peter,' said Ruth with relief when she heard the news. 'He *is* precious! In a way!'

'"Good old Naomi", you should say,' commented Naomi, 'I could have kept the money; it was my magazine! You'll have to think of something better.'

'I know.'

CHAPTER FOUR

Dear Sponsor,

    I am happy to write again to a new sponsor. I am very happy to write to you.

    We write the letters in class, in school. Long letters or short letters, we can choose. The youngest students draw pictures for their sponsors, but I like to write.

    I have seen your small country of England on the map on the classroom wall. I have seen London and Manchester which is where Manchester United are from. Everybody knows Manchester United here.

    Have you seen my country on a map? It is good here. We have no problems in this area. I hope you have no problems in your area.

    I am well. I am going on well with my studies. My favourite is maths and football and English. I have studied English for three years. That is how I can write to you. I like to learn a new language. Now I have three languages, my home language, Swahili, English. Next I may learn French. Many languages

*are spoken in my country. Are many languages spoken
with you?*

*At our place we grow vegetables. We have goats and
some hens. My father works building. At home he built
from wood a new small house for the goats. They stand
on the roof, jump up, jump down. I think they
laugh at us.*

Many books are waiting for me to read.

And so I will stop writing.

Your new friend, Joseck

Even in ordinary years, February was a month that stretched
the girls' resources to their limits.

'Three birthdays *and* a boy to sponsor!' said Naomi,
sighing.

'I'm not bothering with Phoebe's birthday unless she takes
me out of the zoo,' Ruth replied.

'Neither will I, then,' agreed Naomi.

'Neither will you what?' asked Rachel.

'Bother with Phoebe's birthday unless she takes us out of
the zoo.'

'I won't either then,' said Rachel.

'Are you in there, too?'

'I got put in yesterday. She made another cage, just for me.
You go and look, it's awful.'

There were now three cages lined up on the living room
windowsill. Ruth and Naomi glared through the bars of one.
Another contained cardboard figures of Phoebe's teacher and

the Lollipop Lady (recognizable by her Lollipop). 'Not Tame Yet' read their description. In the third was Rachel, all alone and unkindly labelled, 'The Slege Monster'.

'See?' said Rachel.

'What did you do?'

'Nothing, she just hates my sledge, that's all.'

'Did it fall on her in the night again?'

Rachel did not answer, but rattled the bars of her cage rather moodily.

'Well, you don't have to do anything,' said Naomi, 'I didn't. I just got put in for no reason at all.'

'You laughed about the pushchair pushing!' said a voice through a crack in the door. 'You said sardines had tails. And you have been ROBBING MY TRAIN! I saw you!'

Phoebe appeared, clutching her train and a tin-opener. 'With a knitting needle! You know you were!'

'I was only seeing if anything would come out.'

'Did anything?'

'No.'

'Lucky for you,' said Phoebe ominously. 'I heard you talking about my birthday.'

'We're not bothering about your birthday unless you let us out of the zoo,' said Ruth.

'I won't.' Phoebe continued to fish down the slot of her train with the bottle-opener bit of the tin-opener. Tiny bits of paper came up on the hook.

'You'll chop that ten pound note to pieces if you're not

careful,' warned Naomi. 'You're probably squashing it further and further in. Let me have a go.'

Phoebe handed her train over to Naomi, who poked and poked and achieved nothing.

'What about the vacuum cleaner?' suggested Ruth. 'It might suck it out.'

It did not suck it out; they tried for an hour before they gave up, at the end of which Phoebe evidently felt more kindly towards her sisters. She did not let them out of the zoo, but she fed them bits of biscuit through the bars and made them cotton wool nests. Martin came round while they were admiring them, took one look, and said rashly that Phoebe obviously had a personality problem. Phoebe tore out of the room to look for a box.

'Now she's gone,' said Martin to Ruth, 'will you come round and look at Peter and tell me if Phoebe did anything like he's doing now?'

It did not sound a very tempting invitation, but it was another opportunity to make herself indispensable to Peter, and so Ruth agreed.

'Did she do that?' asked Martin, ushering Ruth into the Collingwoods' large and gleaming kitchen.

'Oh yes,' said Ruth, looking in at Peter. 'That sort of thing, anyway.'

Peter, strapped in his high chair, was covered in butter and crumbs, beating his fists as hard as he could on his blue plastic table. Under the fists were crumbs that had been crisps, and all over the floor were more crumbs, a feeding cup, evidently hurled there, his bunny rabbit plate, his shoes and his socks.

'I started him off with his tea,' said Martin. 'Mum asked me to because she's up in her office telephoning and in a minute she has to dash out. But look!'

'Does she always get so much ready?' asked Ruth, catching sight of the stack of miniature egg sandwiches, the salad and apple and cubes of cheese, still waiting on the dresser. It looked an awful lot for a two-year-old.

'Oh no,' said Martin, 'only when she knows I'll have to feed him. It takes such a lot to get any in.'

'What does he do when you give him a sandwich?'

'I'll show you.'

Peter grabbed the sandwich, ripped it in half, squeezed it through his fists, chewed his knuckles, flung one handful on to the floor, hammered the rest flat on his tray, licked up the remains, and turned and dribbled them over the edge.

'Did Phoebe do that?' asked Martin.

'Sometimes. Don't tell her I said so, though.'

'What did you do?'

'Mum used to say, "Right then, we'll fetch Rachel!"'

'What did Rachel do?'

'Well, she ate everything.'

'Even the screwed-up bits?'

'Oh yes, usually.'

Martin looked at Peter's screwed-up bits and shuddered. 'I'm not.'

'No, but it's the right idea. We should take everything away, and tidy up, just as if he'd had it.'

Peter watched in horror as they cleaned the floor, wiped down his chair, washed his hands and arms and elbows and face and head ('Good job he hasn't got much hair,' commented Ruth) and removed the food from sight. He opened his mouth and howled.

'Very nice sandwiches,' said Ruth, taking one out of the fridge and eating it. 'Have one too.'

Martin obediently took one while Peter stared in disbelief.

'Yum!' said Martin.

'Yum!' agreed Ruth, took another, cut it in half, ate one piece herself and, put the other on Peter's tray. Peter made a grab for it, but Ruth got there faster.

'That's what Rachel used to do to Phoebe.' She put another corner of sandwich on Peter's tray and let him get it first. He stuffed it into his mouth as if he was starving.

'See,' said Ruth, rather smugly, 'only you mustn't let him think you want him to eat it.' She ate two more pieces herself before she let Peter grab another. 'He watches you just like Josh does,' she remarked, giving him a bit of cheese. 'Good old Peter,' she added, producing another when it was gone, 'Have a bit more. Food tastes better when you have to fight for it!' and she ate one of his apple slices to prove her point.

'Try him with a whole sandwich,' said Martin.

Ruth did, and he ate it in two starving bites while she took a pretend swig out of his mug and passed it to Martin who obligingly took one too.

'Brilliant,' said Martin, as Peter nearly suffocated himself draining it dry before they could get any more. Mrs Collingwood came in to the astonishing sight of a clean kitchen and her younger son clutching the last sandwich tight in both hands and glaring at Ruth as he consumed it.

'Look what Ruth's made him do!' said Martin.

'Ruth, you're a hero!' Mrs Collingwood exclaimed. 'Fancy you knowing how to manage him. And he's so clean,' she added kissing Peter's bald head, 'compared to what we're used to, I mean! You should see the state of him usually!'

'She did,' said Martin, 'we cleared it up.'

'So useful,' continued Mrs Collingwood, unstrapping Peter and turning him loose on the kitchen floor, where he grovelled round looking for crumbs. 'Could we ask you again sometime? Say, a pound a time, food thrown in, so to speak?'

Ruth stared at her, speechless. She had never imagined it would be so easy. Out of the corner of her eye she saw Martin watching her hopefully.

'It would only be now and then, say once or twice a week. Martin would be here, moral support, if nothing else! Do say yes!'

'Oh yes!' said Ruth.

'I'll have a word with your mother, if you like, although I'm sure she won't mind. Right then, Peter, bath time. Would you like to help, Ruth?'

'No!' said Ruth hastily, 'I mean yes, but it'll be tea-time at home, I'd better go. Oh no,' she added, seeing Mrs Collingwood reach for her purse, 'today can be a free sample!'

'Rubbish,' said Mrs Collingwood, gathering up Peter, 'I have to pay you, you might never come back otherwise!'

'I've got a job,' announced Ruth happily at tea-time, 'feeding Peter, a pound a meal!'

'Did you ask?' asked Mrs Conroy sternly, 'or did they offer?'

'They offered,' replied Ruth proudly, 'they begged!'

'Ask if you have to wear your own clothes,' said Mr Conroy solemnly. 'I've seen that young man with an ice cream. Shocking!'

Naomi waited until she and Ruth were alone together before she said, 'Do you realise that you will have to feed Peter more than a hundred times to get ten pounds a month for a year? That's once every three days! They'll never want you so often.'

'There's pocket money too.'

'There's all the birthdays this month.'

'Homemade for Rachel and Phoebe,' said Ruth firmly, 'and flowers and we'll make a birthday cake for Mum to surprise her. She'll like that.'

Mrs Conroy did like it, but when it came to Rachel's birthday, she demanded explanations.

'What is it?'

'It's a sledge case!'

'I've never seen one before. There's no such thing!'

It was made from an ancient stripy sheet. It looked like a huge bag with straps. So that there should be no doubt as to its use, Ruth and Naomi had embroidered 'Sledge Case' on it in loopy chain stitch.

'I s'pose it's all right if it fits,' said Rachel gracelessly.

'Of course it fits!' replied Ruth crossly. 'D'you think we didn't measure? You might be more grateful; we sewed until our fingers bled, making it!'

'I don't want it if it's bled on,' said Rachel.

'What are you going to get me?' asked Phoebe. 'I don't want a sledge case!'

'Nothing if you're going to be as nasty as Rachel,' said Naomi.

'I'm not being nasty,' argued Rachel, 'I'm being honest!'

Phoebe's turn to ask, 'What is it?' came a few days later.

'It's a zoo keeper's hat!'

'What's the toothbrush for?'

'Cleaning out the cages.'

'What's the cardboard animals for?'

'Putting in the zoo instead of us.'

Phoebe let the cardboard animals loose in the garden and kept her relations in the cages.

'Ruth and Naomi have a secret,' said Rachel, 'a money secret!'

Phoebe was not interested. She was engrossed in writing a letter to Big Grandma.

Dear Big Grandma,
    The 10 pond you give me is stuck in trane. By the slit
it cannot breke it cost to much my trane.
    love Phoebe

'What does it mean?' asked Rachel, reading over her sister's shoulder.

'Can't you read?' asked Phoebe impatiently. 'It says my ten pounds is stuck in the train and you can only get money in by the slit and it's no use saying I'll have to break the train because it's too valuable. So can she think of a way of getting it out.'

'It doesn't say that at all,' argued Rachel. 'Anyway, listen to me. Ruth and Naomi have a secret. I think it's to do with money.'

'They haven't got any money,' pointed out Phoebe, 'that's why they gave us such rubbish birthday presents.'

'What are you drawing?'

'My train.'

'It can't be.'

'It's a picture of if you look through the slit at the money I can't reach.'

'They've been asking about my Christmas money,' continued Rachel. 'Good job they don't know where it is. I bet they'd steal it if they could.'

'Where is it?' asked Phoebe. 'Or have you lost it?'

'It's in a safe place,' Rachel said. 'I think,' she added uncertainly, 'I have to keep going to check.'

Mrs Conroy had persuaded Rachel to deposit her money in a Post Office savings account. 'A special children's one,' Mrs Conroy had said. 'They'll take care of it until you think of something you really want.'

'I really want another huge box of chocolates. Mine's gone

already,' Rachel had remarked, where upon Mrs Conroy had hurried her off to the Post Office without further delay. The disadvantage of the system was that Rachel did not trust the Post Office staff.

'They've only given me this book,' she said, scrutinizing her account. 'They write in it themselves. They could write anything. How do I know they haven't spent it?'

Already Rachel's account book was filling up with a list of deposits and withdrawals, all for the same amount, as Rachel checked up on her money.

'She only wants to look at it,' Mrs Conroy explained the first time Rachel dragged her back. Nevertheless, only four days after having deposited her money, before Rachel could hold it again in her hands, a form signed by Mrs Conroy and Rachel needed to be filled in. Even then, Rachel, receiving her ten pound note, had taken one look and exclaimed,

'That's not mine! Mine was a new one and had a bent corner!'

'So it was,' agreed the cashier, who at that time thought Rachel quite sweet, and he replaced it with a new, bent-cornered one. After examining it carefully, Rachel and her mother filled in another form and handed it back. Since then they had filled in so many forms that a separate pile was kept for Rachel. The Post Office was only round the corner from home and recently she had taken to popping in alone on her way back from school, in order to see the cashier wave a ten pound note at her to prove that, in her brief absence, he had not spent it.

'Catch the public young,' the manager told his staff, 'and you've got them for life.' Whether or not they wanted Rachel for life was a different matter.

'Everyone has money secrets,' remarked Phoebe. 'Ruth and Naomi, Mum and Dad, everyone. You do.'

'How do you know?' Rachel, alarmed, clasped the flat place on her stomach where her Post Office account book was warmly stowed between T-shirt and skin.

Phoebe finished off her letter with a lot of kisses and did not reply.

'I hate it,' said Rachel passionately, 'when people have secrets. It's not fair, it makes me ill. People ought to be made to tell me things.'

'I showed you my letter.'

'It was boring,' said Rachel ungratefully. 'Ruth and Naomi are upstairs writing boring letters too. Secret, boring letters.'

'How do you know?'

'They won't let me in.'

Joseck's letter had arrived the previous morning.

'It's taken weeks,' said Ruth. 'I ought to write back straight away, it's been so long coming.'

'Look,' said Naomi, 'it was my money you sent as well; both of us should write, and we should tell him there's two of us, not just you.'

'I thought you didn't want to share.'

56

'I do now,' said Naomi. Quite suddenly, the letter from Africa had brought Joseck alive. A real person, playing football, reading books, asking questions.

'Three languages,' they read, astonished. 'Manchester United! Maths! His favourite is Maths!'

'I said he looked clever!' said Naomi.

'Look, he's drawn a picture,' discovered Ruth.

Sure enough, at the bottom of the page, in faint pencil lines, a small animal stood on a small sloping roof.

'It's one of his goats!' said Naomi.

'And it's laughing!'

Suddenly, they could not wait to write back.

Dear Joseck,

Thank you for your letter. There are two of us, not just one. Ruth and Naomi. We are sisters. We are both well and we hope you are too. It is cold and wet and dark in our country. We liked your goat. Our father makes things too. He made a sledge for the snow and he is going to make a gate.

We have read about Africa and we found your country, Kenya, on a map. We would like to go there. We would like to see the wild animals, there are not many wild animals here. Do you have sisters or brothers? What books do you read? If we write to you and you write to us, then we can visit each other by letters.

Love from Ruth and Naomi

There was a thumping on the stairs and the door opened and it was Rachel.

'Mrs Collingwood says would Ruth stop with Peter for half an hour while she collects Martin from football?'

'Good!' exclaimed Ruth, jumping up. 'Another pound!'

'I'll post our letter,' said Naomi.

'What letter?' asked Rachel, who was lingering in the hope of discovering secrets. 'What do you spend the money on?'

'Private.'

'I've got a secret,' said Rachel, 'a money secret, too! Don't you want to know what it is?' She was very pleased when Ruth and Naomi turned back eagerly to look at her.

'I knew you would,' she remarked smugly, and disappeared down into the kitchen, where Mrs Conroy was making cakes for Sunday Tea. A baking tray full of small chocolate buns stood on the table, waiting to go into the oven.

'I'd rather have one raw,' said Rachel, looking at them, 'than anything in the world. Than a hundred cooked ones! When will you have time to go to the Post Office with me?'

'Would you rather have one raw than go to the Post Office?' asked her mother. 'Say, for a whole month?'

'For a week anyway.'

'A month.'

'Two weeks,' said Rachel, edging towards the table.

'Three weeks.'

'Three weeks then,' agreed Rachel. 'Do you think it will be safe that long?'

'Didn't you read that little book the man at the Post Office gave you? All about how they look after your money?'

'I read it in the bath.'

'Yes?'

'But I dropped it in before I could believe it. That's why I have to keep checking.'

'Well, you'll have to wait three weeks, now you've eaten that cake.'

'Six weeks if you give me another,' offered Rachel, and was ordered out of the kitchen.

CHAPTER FIVE

In the Post Office window there was a notice board, full of adverts for jobs.

'Experienced Nanny, also willing to cook and exercise dogs. Own car essential. Weekends and evenings as necessary. Typist preferred. References required.' That card had been there so long that it was brown at the edges, and so had the one that read, 'Cheerful young man to service, maintain and repair pensioner's car in return for occasional use.'

Naomi, pausing at the window after posting Joseck's letter, noticed a new card in the list:

'Reliable gardener required.

2–3 hours per week.

Tools provided.

Previous applicant need not reapply.'

Naomi, wondering what the previous applicant had done to receive such a public rebuke, wrote down the address.

'How much d'you think gardeners get paid?' she asked Martin the next morning.

'Depends on their qualifications, I should think.'

'If they haven't got any qualifications?'

'Well, depends on their experience then, I suppose.'

'If they haven't any of that either?'

'Who'd employ them, then?' asked Martin practically.

Somebody might, Naomi thought hopefully. She had spent the summer gardening at Big Grandma's house in the north, and found that it was something she enjoyed. That evening after school she cycled away to inspect the address. Nothing could have been more disheartening. A shabby red brick bungalow, surrounded by concrete paths and empty flower-beds. As Naomi looked, a curtain moved and a face appeared at the window.

'Looking for someone?' asked a voice behind her, and Naomi turned to see Mrs Reed, her old primary school headmistress.

'Naomi, isn't it?' she enquired. 'Phoebe and Rachel's sister. I never forget a face! What are you doing here?'

'Just looking at the garden. It needs gardening.'

'It certainly does,' agreed Mrs Reed. 'Nothing to redeem it, except that old apple tree.'

For the first time, Naomi noticed a huge old apple tree that stooped across one corner of the garden. Beneath it was a garden shed, so old that the wood had weathered to a silver greyness.

'And the shed.'

'Yes,' agreed Mrs Reed, slightly surprised. 'Anyway, I'm afraid it's all beyond the old couple these days.'

The front door of the bungalow had opened and an ancient man, swaying between two sticks, made his way along the garden path towards them. He did not, Naomi noticed with disappointment, look rich.

'I see you looking,' he called from half-way up the path, 'and I knowed what you come for.'

'To see the garden,' explained Naomi, shouting in case he was deaf. 'I saw your card in the Post Office.'

'Are you one of Linda's?' he asked, looking across at Mrs Reed.

'One of mine grown up a bit,' agreed Mrs Reed. 'I didn't realize you were thinking of tackling the garden yourself, Naomi?'

'I like gardens,' said Naomi.

'That's good to hear. Have you met Toby and Emma?'

'She've just met Toby,' said Toby, smiling a toothless smile at Naomi, 'and Emma's on her way. Emma's slowed down a bit these days,' he continued, 'she can't get about like she did. She'm dead set on having the garden planted up, though. Here she comes for a look.'

Glancing behind him, Naomi saw an old lady progressing along the path with such small footsteps that she seemed to drift. The March breeze that chased last year's dead leaves in circles through the garden seemed more than likely to sweep her away with them. With a voice like paper in the wind she remarked,

'I was one of the first Girl Guides!'

'Oh,' said Naomi, and then, rather stupidly, 'Why did you leave?'

Emma did not seem to find it a stupid question. 'I wonder now,' she admitted, 'perhaps I shouldn't have rushed off.'

'This young lady,' announced Toby, 'is our new gardener! And a cut above the last, if you ask me!'

'Cheeky young devil, him,' remarked Emma.

'Well, it looks like you've got the job,' said Mrs Reed to Naomi. 'Do you want me to have a word with your mother? I've known Toby and Emma for years. I'll give you my number and you can tell her to give me a call. Or she can pop into my office when she's collecting your sisters. How would that be? All right?'

'Yes, yes thank you,' Naomi managed to say, still looking in astonishment at the empty, dusky garden, the goblin figures of the old people, and Mrs Reed, who seemed to think there was nothing unusual in the situation.

'Pound an hour,' said Toby, suddenly business-like. 'No radios, no acting unreasonable, and no digging up of Roger!'

'Who's Roger?' asked Naomi, completely bemused.

'Him that come before,' Emma told her, 'dug him up!'

'Upset them terribly,' said Mrs Reed. 'Roger was their parrot!'

Suddenly Naomi realized that the garden had a third feature. Apple tree, silver shed, grave marked with a wooden cross.

'We could grow flowers on him,' she suggested, 'parrot-coloured! Red and yellow and bright green and blue.'

'Shallow-rooted,' breathed Emma.

'One of Linda's,' said Toby, who seemed to think a great deal of Mrs Reed. 'One of Linda's got the job. Come back Saturday, any time Saturday.'

'I'll make sure I speak to your mother before then,' said Mrs Reed. 'I've written down my number for you. Here!'

'Thank you,' said Naomi again.

Toby's hands were shaking on his sticks.

'Get into the warm,' Mrs Reed ordered him. 'You too, Naomi! I hope that bike has proper lights!'

Naomi nodded but did not move, waiting to see her employers safely indoors. Mrs Reed gave her arm a friendly pat.

'We'll all be old one day,' she told her. 'Well into their nineties, those two are. We'll be lucky if we're as bright as they are when it comes to our turn!'

Naomi, cycling home, thought about that.

'One day you'll be old,' she told Phoebe when she got in.

'I shan't!'

'Ninety!'

'I won't!'

'Older than Big Grandma!'

Phoebe said nothing, busy rolling plasticine. 'Mrs Collingwood,' she said proudly, showing Naomi a plasticine person she had already made. 'I told her I was a vegetarian and she called me a sausage! She'll have to live in Phoebe's cage till I find another box. I'm making plasticine sausages for her tea. Serve her right!'

Rachel came wandering in and was introduced to the latest

victim. 'Mrs Collingwood in with me?' she asked. 'Brilliant! I hated being on my own!'

Naomi spent the evening reading her father's gardening catalogues and making a list of all the red, yellow and blue plants that might be suitable for a parrot's grave.

'How deep is he buried?' asked Ruth, when the situation had been explained to her.

'Not very, I shouldn't think, if they had to dig the hole themselves.'

'Wonder how long he's been dead,' mused Ruth. 'Pity to waste him, really!'

'If I dig up Roger for you,' said Naomi sternly, 'I'll get the sack!'

'Yes, all right,' said Ruth hastily. 'Probably too late anyway! Fancy you being a reliable gardener! You've only ever grown those radishes and things at Big Grandma's!'

'Well, she said they turned out very nicely,' said Naomi. 'Anyway, I did a lot of other things too. Digging and weeding, you know I did! Anyway, anyone can garden, thousands of books tell you how. It's not as bad as being a baby-sitter who's only practised on Phoebe! You can't look up babies in books!'

'You can,' replied Ruth serenely. 'I did in the library. There's all sorts of ways of bringing them up – depends what you want them to grow up like!'

'What do you do with Peter, then?'

'Whatever stops him screaming quickest,' said Ruth.

Mrs Reed spoke to Mrs Conroy as she had promised, explaining that Naomi had arranged to do some gardening for a nice old couple she knew well.

'We've been neighbours for years,' she said, 'and I'm very fond of them. It will brighten them wonderfully to have a young person about. And I gather Naomi likes gardening.'

'She got interested last summer,' admitted Mrs Conroy. 'I don't see why she shouldn't try and help them out, I suppose.'

'Perhaps you'd go and see them yourself,' Mrs Reed suggested, and Mrs Conroy replied that she would, as soon as she had time. Mr Conroy, seeing Naomi poring over his garden catalogues, offered to help with ideas.

'I'll ask if I'm stuck,' said Naomi, not feeling stuck at all.

By Friday evening her plans were complete, and if all went as she hoped, Toby and Emma's red brick bungalow was well on the way to being transformed. Ruth, nobly sacrificing several nights' homework to a good cause, had painted pictures illustrating the blossomy paradise her sister intended to create. During spring and summer the bungalow would be entirely lost beneath garlands of honeysuckle and roses. The autumn scene showed an odd brick or two peering from between golden leaves, but winter restored the old outlines completely, softened only by deep snow, ivy and glowing windows.

'There!' said Ruth.

'There!' said Naomi on Saturday afternoon, plonking down her sister's pictures on Toby's knee.

'We must be quiet!' whispered Toby, nodding across to the armchair where Emma lay sleeping, almost obscured by cushions and rugs. Creakingly, he rose and shuffled across the room to blot out Emma altogether with another piece of blanket.

'Bring your pictures,' he told Naomi, and led her to the ice-cold kitchen. Naomi followed, after tiptoeing across the room to see that Emma had not been extinguished completely by her coverings. Toby sat at the kitchen table and carefully spread the paintings out before him.

'Well? What do you think?' asked Naomi.

'Very bright and pretty,' said Toby eventually, 'but to be honest, my dear . . .' he glanced up and saw Naomi's face.

'If you'd ha' brought me these,' he continued, 'say, twenty, twenty-five years ago I'd have snapped these pictures up, and should Emma have wanted a garden so bad like she suddenly do now, I'd have planted the lot!'

'Good,' said Naomi, 'but what about now?'

'Twenty-five years ago,' said Toby firmly.

'I wasn't here twenty-five years ago,' said Naomi impatiently, 'I was minus thirteen!'

'Emma and me was seventy each,' Toby told her mildly. 'I tell you frankly, my dear, these roses and trees take such a time to grow, you wouldn't believe.'

There was a silence.

'Time you wouldn't believe,' he repeated, as Naomi bundled the pictures together and marched towards the door.

'Well, why'd you want a gardener, then?' she demanded.

'What we need is fast flowers,' continued Toby, producing a pencil and a bit of paper from the kitchen drawer. 'Fast flowers! Straight from the packet and up in weeks! Annuals, you can scatter them anywhere and they flower all summer. What about that?'

'S'pose it's your garden,' said Naomi ungraciously, 'but I'd grow roses and honeysuckle and stuff.'

'So would I,' agreed Toby, 'so would I. But you write these things down for me now. Six-week stocks and them nasturtiums that climb everywhere and poppies aren't fussy, and them big blue morning glory things that grow up quick and bright, you make a list and nip into town for the seeds and bang 'em in and there we are.'

'What about Ruth's pictures?' asked Naomi, at the end of an afternoon spent choosing the fastest, brightest, toughest seeds in the seed catalogue.

'Emma would love a look at them,' said Toby.

'Even though it won't look like that?'

'It will still look grand, just grand another way.'

'All right,' agreed Naomi, who was beginning to understand.

'How did you get on?' Ruth had arrived to meet her and was waiting impatiently at the garden gate. She pounced on Naomi as she came out.

'He wants the garden packed full of flowers as soon as he can, any old flowers, so long as they're there. He liked your pictures but he said they would take too long.'

'What's he done with them, then?'

'Stuck them up on the kitchen wall.'

'Oh,' said Ruth, as disappointed as Naomi had been, and she did not say anything else as they cycled home together.

'S'pose it's his garden,' she admitted grudgingly, as they wedged their bikes into the garden shed. 'Did you get paid?'

Naomi pulled a ten pound note from her pocket. 'Three for me and the rest for seeds to get us started. I've got a list. I said I'd get them after school. But . . .' Naomi paused.

'What's the matter?'

Naomi, looking very worried, had hunched herself down on to the lawn-mower.

'Their bungalow,' she explained. 'It's freezing cold in the kitchen and dismal in the living room and everything's old and bare. There's nothing cheerful except your pictures, and Toby and Emma are old too. He can't bend down and they walk so slowly . . .' She stopped speaking and stared at the ten pound note. 'I don't think they can afford me. I don't like taking it.'

Ruth lowered herself into a spidery corner, full of trowels and cobwebs and gnawed her knees in thought.

'It's all right for you. The Collingwoods are rich!' said Naomi.

'Too rich,' said Ruth gloomily. 'They're going away for Easter. Italy! Before it gets too crowded! No money for three weeks! And fancy taking Peter to Italy! What a waste! It's not fair.'

'I wouldn't be seen dead with Peter in Italy,' said Naomi.

'Neither would I,' agreed Ruth, cheering up. 'And you know if Toby and Emma want a garden, they have to pay someone. Might as well be you. Anyway, a pound an hour is very cheap, I bet. You cost less than the seeds!'

'S'pose I do.'

'When I can, I'll come and help you and we'll still only be a pound an hour and they'll get even more money's-worth!'

Ruth scrambled to her feet and pulled Naomi out of the lawn-mower box. They trudged indoors, shedding cobwebs and grass cuttings all over the kitchen.

'Where have you been, to get like that?' asked Mrs Conroy.

'Sitting in the shed.'

'Sitting in the shed!' repeated Mrs Conroy, 'and Rachel has just come home covered in dog hairs and says she's been sitting in Josh's basket . . .'

'Only for a minute,' interrupted Rachel.

'It only *took* a minute! Upstairs, all of you, and take the clothes brush! Where's Phoebe disappeared to?'

'Here,' said Phoebe from beneath the kitchen table, where she had been studying Big Grandma's reply to her letter.

Dear Phoebe,

Your train is worth more than ten pounds so if you break it you will be the loser. Therefore, until you have exhausted all possibilities do not break the train. At the moment the train and your money are both safe. I explained your difficulty to Graham and he suggested that you fish down the slit with very sticky chewing gum. He said Good Luck! Let us know how you get on!

Love from Grandma (Big)

Big Grandma's letter was as plain as Phoebe's had been obscure, and Graham had very kindly drawn a picture to illustrate how to fish with chewing gum. As a result, an afternoon's fishing had left Phoebe dreadfully entangled, and with no money at all to show for it. Mrs Conroy, regarding her hands with disgust, ordered her upstairs with her sisters.

'Naomi, turn the taps on for her and make sure she doesn't touch *anything*!' she called after them, 'and make her wash in cold water: hot just makes chewing gum stick worse! I told you to take no notice of that letter, Phoebe! Your grandmother is ridiculous!'

Rachel, waiting her turn for the bathroom while Ruth brushed grass cuttings off Naomi, saw something fall from Naomi's pocket and pounced, but a moment too late.

'Where did you get it?' she asked, as Naomi stuffed the ten pound note back into her jeans. An awful suspicion seized her and hastily she clasped her front and was reassured to find her Post Office book still there. Over the weeks it had softened and moulded so comfortably to the shape of Rachel's stomach that she could no longer feel it. It couldn't be hers, so whose was it? 'It's out of Phoebe's train!' she guessed suddenly.

'WHAT!' exclaimed Phoebe, shooting, bright red and dripping, from the bathroom.

'Of course it isn't,' said Naomi, allowing Phoebe to examine the note. 'Look, yours was folded into squares; this one's nearly new. Anyway, how would I have got it?'

'I don't know,' admitted Phoebe, suddenly gloomy. 'Chewing gum doesn't work.' She pulled out Big Grandma's letter and looked at it again. 'How will I know when all possibilities have been exhausted?'

71

'Course you'll know,' said Rachel, surprised to find herself for once the cleverest, 'your train will be all smashed to pieces!'

Toby was rather astonished the next Saturday to see that his gardening staff had suddenly doubled in size.

'Ruth's just come to read,' Naomi explained, unloading a heap of library books from her bike basket. 'We went to the library and got all these gardening books, so I'm going to garden and she's going to read the instructions.'

'You're a bright lass to think of that,' Toby told her approvingly. 'There's the key to the shed, where you'll find the tools. I must go and get Emma started.'

'Started?'

'Wrapped up, like, to come out and see you. She've been looking at those pictures you made all week.'

He disappeared indoors, leaving Ruth and Naomi to explore the shed, select a spade and bucket, and begin the task of giving Toby his money's-worth.

'Preparation of the ground,' read Ruth, sitting on the upturned bucket. 'The ground should be made ready during the winter months . . .'

'Too late,' said Naomi, 'skip that bit.'

'Liming and fertilizing . . .'

'I don't know what that is, so you'll have to skip that as well.'

'Preliminary digging . . .'

'We haven't got time.'

Ruth turned the pages until she came to 'Laying out a seed-bed, nursery beds and Accelerated seedling production'.

'I'm not bothering with rubbish like that,' said Naomi, busily pulling weeds from around Roger's grave. 'Find where you put the seeds in.'

'It's three chapters,' said Ruth, finding it and settling comfortably on her bucket to read. 'It begins, "One of the advantages of outdoor seed-beds is that they can be prepared and sown by semi-skilled staff . . ."'

'What a cheek,' exclaimed Naomi. 'Semi-skilled! Skip that bit!'

'"The land must be free from weeds, especially the perennial kinds, such as nettles . . ."'

'I'm freeing it,' said Naomi, sitting down hard, as a dandelion unplugged rather quickly. 'Go on a bit!'

'"If drainage is not good . . ."'

'Skip that, we couldn't do anything about it anyway.'

'"Autumn sowing", might as well skip that. What a useless book; I've skipped nearly all of it! You bash out the lumps while I pull the weeds up, that'll be twice as quick!'

By the time Toby and Emma appeared, they had finished one border and were ripping open packets of cornflowers and poppies and scattering the seeds.

'Save the marigolds for Roger,' Naomi reminded Ruth, 'and I bought some runner beans out of my own money, to climb up the wall behind him.' Emma, sitting on the chair Toby had brought out for her, nodded approvingly. 'Nice and bright,' she said, 'but shallow-rooted! I don't forget!'

'No,' said Naomi, extremely surprised.

'I was one of the first Girl Guides, you know,' Emma continued, 'I should never have left! You were right!'

'I was one of the last,' said Ruth cheerfully.

'One of the last?'

'Well, I got thrown out!'

This remark startled Emma so much that she looked several years younger.

'Got thrown out?' she repeated.

'For bandaging,' Ruth told her. 'We had to do bandaging and I bandaged someone's legs together and bandaged them to the table . . .'

'Shut up!' whispered Naomi.

'Well, it was only Egg-Yolk Wendy,' said Ruth unrepentently, 'and when I'd bandaged her to the table she went on and on so much I bandaged her mouth shut . . .'

Naomi glanced up from her weeding to see how Emma was taking these remarks and then bent down again, reassured. Emma, sighing and bowing on the kitchen chair, appeared to be laughing.

Two weeks later the garden was transformed, dug and weeded and planted with seeds. Already, with not a single leaf or seedling showing, it looked a very different place from the neglected patch that Naomi had first visited. Between pocket money and Peter and gardening, Joseck's money had been earned twice over.

'We ought to keep the spare money for next month,' said Ruth.

'We needn't,' said Naomi airily, 'we can always earn more. The Collingwoods will be back in a couple of weeks and that garden will always need gardening.'

It was too tempting; it was so long since they had had any money to spend. The shops were full of Easter eggs; in one you could wait while they iced a person's name on the egg of your choice. Egg-Yolk Wendy, clutching the unfortunate Gavin by the arm, was waiting in the queue.

'Gavin's getting my name put on an egg,' she told them, smirking.

'Poor you,' remarked Ruth 'can't you stop him?'

'Not very kind of you, Gavin,' added Naomi.

'I suppose,' said Ruth, 'it's nothing actually to be ashamed of.'

Wendy let go of Gavin's arm and looked at him uncertainly. Gavin, hovering on one leg in the doorway, glanced at his rescuers with sudden hope.

'We've come to get one done for our little sisters,' explained Ruth. 'Rachel's too old really, but she only sulks if she doesn't get the same as Phoebe.'

'She's immature,' said Naomi, but Wendy had already disappeared.

Ruth moved to the front of the queue and said, 'We want one egg with Mum and Dad on it please, and another with Rachel written on one half and Phoebe on the other.'

'It'll look all wrong in the box.'

'They won't care about the box,' said Naomi cheerfully. 'And one of those little pink rabbits with Gavin on please!'

'We don't normally ice rabbits,' said the girl, 'but I'll do it anyway for a favour! That poor lad! I was watching through the window. She counted his money and dragged him inside!'

'I wonder,' said Naomi as they walked home, 'if they have Easter in Africa.'

'Well, they have Christmas.'

'They must have, then. Look! There's Gavin and Wendy! Give me that rabbit!'

Ruth handed it to her, and distracted Wendy by the simple remark, 'Your hair's growing out at the roots,' while Naomi planted the rabbit in Gavin's school bag, where it was discovered with rage and suspicion by Wendy the next morning.

'I bet they don't have chocolate Easter eggs though,' continued Naomi as if no interruption had occurred. 'I wonder if Joseck's got our letter yet? I wish they didn't take so long to get there.'

'Perhaps he's reading it now,' said Ruth, guessing exactly right.

Dear Ruth and Naomi,

I am glad to be your friend.

Here are the answers to your questions.

I have one brother. He works with my father. I have no sisters, but a little cousin, Mari.

The animals we have are six goats and the chickens. In the hills there are deer and small cats and foxes and others I have not seen. The books I read are about many things. Science and other countries and sports. Here it not cold, like you have, but we have a fire at night sometimes. What are you doing in your country? Here we have already harvested beans. The boys in my class play football and Mari comes to play too. She is too small and we say no but she still comes.

I am very happy to have your letter.

Your friend in Kenya, Joseck

CHAPTER SIX

Rachel and Phoebe woke up at five o'clock on Easter morning and discovered, to their huge delight, that the Easter bunny had left his presents on the end of their beds.

'Which will never happen again,' said Mrs Conroy, later that disastrous day.

'*We* were all right,' pointed out Rachel.

Between five o'clock and half-past six that morning, Rachel and Phoebe consumed three large chocolate eggs, one packet of marzipan ducks, one packet of peppermint cream rabbits, three bananas taken from the kitchen for no good reason that Rachel could give, two hard-boiled eggs, painted pink with their names on, and two cooking apples, raw, because they were thirsty. Strengthened by their efforts, and finding there was nothing left to eat, they went to see how Ruth and Naomi were getting on.

Naomi was lying very curled up on the edge of her bed, clutching the pillow with one hand and looking strangely pale.

'Happy Easter!' said Rachel, bouncing on to her feet,

'thanks for your Easter egg; we ate half each. Here's yours from me, home-made at school.' She pulled an oily parcel from her dressing gown pocket. 'It's made of coconut ice. We could do six little ones or one big one so I did you one big one! And Phoebe made one for Ruth.'

'Where's Ruth?' demanded Phoebe. 'She didn't find her Easter egg. I hid it for a surprise for her up Old Teddy's jumper and I've just looked and it's still there!'

'She must have slept with it all night,' remarked Rachel. 'Is it squashed?'

'Just a bit melted!'

Naomi had unwrapped her parcel and was gazing at a large greyish egg, splashed all over with paintbox-red dots.

'We decorated them last night,' said Rachel complacently. 'Taste it!'

Naomi broke off the smallest possible crumb.

'Hurry up, it's lovely!'

'In a minute!' snapped Naomi, so fiercely Rachel and Phoebe stared in surprise.

'She's in a mood,' said Phoebe, and when Ruth pushed the door open and collapsed on to her bed, she asked, 'Are you in a mood too?'

'Shut up. Go away,' said Ruth, and pulled her pillow over her head. Naomi pulled it away again to ask, 'Were you?'

'No.'

'We've eaten all our Easter stuff,' Rachel told Ruth. 'We had a feast; we didn't mean to, but then it didn't seem worth stopping so we ate the hard-boiled eggs and ducks and rabbits that Big Grandma sent, to finish!'

'Look under Old Teddy's jumper, Ruth,' said Phoebe. 'I've put a surprise!'

'Something in this room smells disgusting,' said Ruth, not listening. 'Really sweet and disgusting, I've been smelling it all night.'

Phoebe lost patience and banged Old Teddy down on Ruth's stomach so hard that he laid an egg, damp and rather hairy. It was suddenly too much for Ruth.

'Where are they?' asked Mrs Conroy, coming in a few moments later to see what all the noise was about.

'Both in the bathroom,' Rachel told her.

'What have they been eating?'

'Nothing, well, Naomi ate a bit of the Easter egg we made her. Ruth wouldn't even look at hers, she shouted, "Get it out of my bed! Get it out of my bed!" and ran to the bathroom, and then Naomi ran after her!'

'And are you two all right?'

'Very all right,' said Rachel, taking a bite of Ruth's egg to prove it.

Except for a temporary loss of appetite at breakfast time, both Rachel and Phoebe continued to be all right. Ruth and Naomi spent the day in bed.

'Tummy upsets,' said Mrs Conroy, and ordered Rachel and Phoebe to stay out of the way. However, Rachel visited the invalids on Monday morning and returned looking pleased with herself.

'I've taken their Easter eggs to look after,' she told Phoebe.

'Do they know?' asked Phoebe.

'I didn't tell them because they hate talking about food so much.'

When they weren't any better by Tuesday the doctor came and said, 'Gastric flu. Lucky the other two have escaped.'

'Escaped what?' asked Rachel.

'Catching what your big sisters have gone down with,' said the doctor, who was an old friend of Rachel's. 'Stick your tongue out. Give me your wrist, jump up and down a bit, say "Ah!"'

'Ah! Ah! Am I all right?' demanded Rachel.

'Sound as a bell,' said the doctor, handing Mrs Conroy a sheaf of prescriptions. 'And how's Phoebe, the wonder child? Still top of the class?'

'Yes,' said Phoebe, not very modestly. 'Do you think I have gastric flu?'

'Not noticeably,' said the doctor.

'How much longer do you think it's going to last?' asked Naomi wearily on Thursday. Her head was hot and thumping and her back was shaking cold and when she tried to write a note to Toby, she found herself going dizzy.

Dear Toby and Emma,
*   I am sorry we have not been but we have flu. Will*
come as soon as we can.
*   Love, Naomi and Ruth*

It took her all afternoon, in bits and pieces, to write it. Ruth, staggering out of bed to look for a stamp, suddenly slipped and bashed her head on the windowsill.

'Are you getting better?' asked Phoebe, through a crack in the door.

'I don't think so,' said Ruth. 'Will you post a letter for us?'

'Has it got germs on?'

'Probably.'

'Wait,' commanded Phoebe, and came back wearing her winter mittens as protection.

'The doctor said it wasn't the paint we put on your eggs,' she said, grabbing the letter and going out again very quickly.

'No, I know.'

'And the egg up Old Teddy's jumper couldn't have made anyone as sick as this.'

'No.'

'I'm sorry, but me and Rachel have sort of eaten your Easter eggs.'

'Oh well,' said Ruth, 'we knew you probably would. Go and borrow Josh, so Martin doesn't forget he said we could share him, and post this letter for us.'

'They've all gone to Italy and poor Josh is in kennels.'

'Oh yes, I forgot.'

'Mum said we'd go to the park after lunch,' said Phoebe. 'We'll post it on the way. We're taking bubbles because it's lovely and windy. When are you going to get better?'

Ruth said she didn't know. It felt like they'd been ill for months. However, by the weekend they had progressed to dry toast and orange juice and could sit up and read without feeling that their heads might explode at any minute. The next day they staggered downstairs and managed scrambled eggs for tea.

'You look a pair of little ghosts,' remarked Mr Conroy.

'You've wasted all the holidays,' said Phoebe, 'school again on Monday.'

'Not for these two,' said their mother. 'They're going up to Grandma's for a few days of fresh air! They're still far from fit for school; they'd pick up the first thing that was going around.'

'It's not fair,' said Rachel bitterly that afternoon in the garden. 'You two always leave me and Phoebe out of everything!'

'We don't!'

'You do. You're getting all stuck-up and bossy. Aren't they, Phoebe?'

'Like Egg-Yolk Wendy,' agreed Phoebe.

'WE'RE NOT!'

'You didn't care that we ate your Easter eggs! You were poorly without us and now you're going to sneak off to Big Grandma's and we'll be left behind! You even write letters to people we don't know, and,' concluded Rachel, gratified to find that real tears of frustration were rolling down her cheeks, 'you've had a huge, great big money secret without us for ages now! It's not fair!'

Naomi stared at Rachel in amazement and remarked briefly that she was cracked.

'Yes, you are,' agreed Ruth. 'We're only going to Big Grandma's because we were ill. You could have come and caught it if you'd wanted to! You never came near us, except to pinch our Easter eggs!'

'I didn't know about missing school and going to Big Grandma's then,' said Rachel, sniffing.

'And how do you know we've got money secrets? And if we had, why should we tell you? You'd tell everyone and you wouldn't help!'

'I would!' Another tear trickled down Rachel's face and she wiped her nose on her knees and tried to look pathetic.

'You would what?' asked Naomi suddenly. 'Help? Or tell everyone?' Once again she and Ruth were worrying about Joseck's money. It was obvious that very little, if any, could be earned that month. Two weeks had gone already and all their savings had been spent on the Easter eggs.

'I wouldn't tell anyone,' said Rachel hopefully, 'I would help. Promise!'

'Promise for ever?'

'Promise for ever,' agreed Rachel, her tears drying up like magic.

'What about you, Phoebe?'

'I'll promise not to tell anyone,' agreed Phoebe, who never told anyone anything anyway, 'but,' she added cautiously, 'I don't promise to help!'

'Typical,' said Naomi. 'Anyway, listen.'

Ruth began. About the cold day in the library when she had read about Africa to get warm. About Joseck and his school. About saying she was eighteen when she wasn't. And in between there was Peter and Toby and Emma, goats on roofs, and chickens. Manchester United and being a sponsor. Halfway through she fetched Joseck's photograph and his letter, and that made it easier.

Then Naomi took over, and explained about the charity that arranged it all, and the ten pounds a month that was so hard to find.

'What will happen if you don't send the money?' asked Phoebe. 'I mean, except for Ruth getting arrested for saying she was eighteen?'

'Oh, thank you for caring,' said Ruth.

'We don't know,' Naomi said. 'Perhaps they'll just tell him we're not bothering any more. Perhaps they might even stop him going to school. Then he will feel awful.'

'He might be glad,' said Rachel. 'I would be.'

'He likes school, he's clever. I bet he'd be miserable. And we're supposed to be his friends.'

'You have to send his money,' said Phoebe firmly, 'or else you will be mean pigs and I will bury your cage in the garden and worms will come and live with you!'

'But we spent all our money on Easter eggs, and then we got ill and we couldn't earn any more and now we've got to go to Big Grandma's,' said Ruth miserably.

'Well, me and Rachel will help,' said Phoebe grandly, ignoring Rachel's alarmed expression. 'You should have asked us before!'

*

Two days later found Rachel staring at the envelope Ruth and Naomi had left behind, and feeling completely unheroic.

'It's addressed and got a stamp on and everything,' Ruth had said. 'All you have to do is put a ten pound postal order inside, or a ten pound note if that's easier.'

Nothing was easy about the task. But it was too late now; Ruth and Naomi were gone, Rachel had promised, and Phoebe's train had refused to yield its riches.

I suppose, thought Rachel, wriggling with horror at the thought, *I suppose I'll have to rob the Post Office.*

It was the only solution she could think of, and because worrying about robbing the Post Office somehow felt even more alarming than actually doing the deed, Rachel stowed Ruth's envelope in her usual hiding place and set off at a nervous trot to commit the crime.

There was a queue at the counter. One position was closed, and at the other, where Rachel's nice cashier was sitting, two old ladies waited to draw their pensions. The cashier recognized Rachel at once and cheerfully waved a ten pound note at her. Pretending not to notice, Rachel lined up behind the old ladies. It would have been comforting to be in disguise, but then the whole success of Rachel's plan depended on the fact that the cashier would know who she was. The first old lady moved away and Rachel's hands tightened on her quaking stomach.

It isn't really crime, she thought, feeling unburglarish, *It's my money. It's not my fault they won't give it to me without a grown-up. They should have told me that, before I put it in. I never would have then; they're the burglars, not me. I'm only getting it back. It's my money!* She found herself standing at the counter and realized she had spoken aloud.

'Of course it is,' agreed the cashier. 'Did you think I'd spent it? There you are,' and he slapped a ten pound note down on his side of the counter.

'That's not mine,' said Rachel, determined to take only what was her own. 'You know it isn't. Mine was much newer and had a bent corner.'

'How could I have forgotten?' asked the cashier, reaching down and producing a new, bent-cornered one. 'There it is!'

Rachel's hand, damp and grubby and cold with fear, but small enough to achieve her purpose, shot beneath the grille, grabbed the ten pound note, and the next moment she was running, running as fast as she could, out of the Post Office, and round the corner to the letter-box that stood at the end of the street. Here she paused and looked back. She had expected to be pursued, but no one had given chase. Hastily she retrieved the envelope from her front, stuffed the ten pound note inside and posted it.

Now Joseck's safe! she thought, and the feeling of relief and achievement was so great that she hugged herself with delight. A second later her happiness left her. If Joseck was safe, it was equally certain that she, Rachel, definitely wasn't. Why hadn't the cashier run after her, she wondered? Or perhaps he had, but she'd been too fast. Perhaps he had simply called the police and they were at her home, waiting for her, or tracking her footsteps with Alsation dogs on leads. Rachel looked down at her dusty trainers and wondered if she should take them off, to baffle the dogs. It seemed a sensible idea.

Cautiously, in her socks, she retraced her footsteps to the corner and looked round. There was the Post Office, she could see the red and yellow sign, but nobody was outside looking for her. Except for two small boys on bikes and a tortoiseshell cat, the street was empty.

No policemen waited for her at the Post Office door. Rachel, tiptoeing past, listened for the sound of voices, unaware that inside, the manager and the cashier were laughing and laughing. They had not called the police, or prepared an ambush or given chase because they had another plan. It was to have a word with Rachel's mother.

Weak with relief, Rachel reached her home and noticed with satisfaction that no police vans were parked outside. It looked unbelievably normal. Her mother was potting up seedlings in the shed.

'I've grown far too many,' she remarked to Rachel, not seeming to notice that her daughter had turned into a criminal. 'Perhaps Naomi will take a few to her old people when she gets back from Big Grandma's.'

It was as if the past hour had been a dream. Mr Conroy sat in his usual chair, reading gloomily through a pile of bills.

'Where's Phoebe?' asked Rachel.

'Upstairs, as far as I know.'

Phoebe was sitting on her bunk bed, looking very guilty. As Rachel entered, she jumped and stuffed something under her pillow.

'I've robbed the Post Office,' said Rachel.

'I've broken my train,' said Phoebe.

There was a small silence while they glared at each other.

'You'll get in awful trouble,' said Rachel, not without a certain amount of satisfaction.

'So will you.'

Side by side they sat on Phoebe's bed and contemplated the tattered remains of the Post Office book, and the shattered china of Phoebe's train.

'Just proves,' remarked Rachel eventually, 'how stupid it is to save money. I never will again. Look what happens!'

'Was it hard, robbing the Post Office?' enquired Phoebe presently.

'Terrible. Horriblest thing I've ever done.'

Phoebe, remembering with awe all the horrible things Rachel had ever done, things which included setting fire to Big Grandma's house and being accidently sick into someone else's desk ('Well, at least it wasn't your own,' Naomi had remarked at the time), shuddered in sympathy.

'You needn't have done it, now I've broken my train.'

'You needn't have broken your train now I've robbed the Post Office.'

'Listen!' said Phoebe.

Downstairs there was a sudden clamour of voices: Mrs Conroy's raised, exclaiming, and Mr Conroy's and at least one stranger's.

'Rachel!' shouted Mrs Conroy up the stairs. 'I think you've got some explaining to do, young lady!'

'Come with me,' begged Rachel, 'before they come up here and see your train.'

'Just keep saying sorry,' advised Phoebe, and, 'Sorry I robbed the Post Office!' said Rachel over and over again, to her dissatisfied parents and the Post Office manager, who had arrived as soon as he was able to manage.

Nothing could persuade her to say any more, to explain why she had done it, or how she had disposed of the money. Backed loyally by Phoebe, she repeated that she was sorry, she wished she hadn't, and she never would do it again.

'Try and cry a bit,' suggested Phoebe, in a whisper that was unfortunately overheard. She was sent from the room, and Rachel, without her support, really did manage to burst into tears – loud, noisy roaring ones, drowning the sound of all further questions.

'What are you doing to her?' enquired Phoebe, returning to the room after concealing the remains of her train.

'Nobody is doing anything to her,' said Mrs Conroy crossly, and eventually they gave up and sent her to bed, where she slept soundly and awoke to a day of bright sunshine and the cheerful thought that the worst was over.

'You're in disgrace,' her father told her.

'I know,' agreed Rachel, staring at her knees, but she did not feel disgraced. She felt noble.

CHAPTER SEVEN

Two days after Ruth and Naomi arrived in Cumbria, a grubby envelope was delivered to them.

> *Dear R and N,*
> *We have don it now.*
> *Love, Phoebe*

Underneath this unreassuring remark, Phoebe, using an enormous amount of black pencil and spit, had drawn a detailed and dramatic picture of recent events in Lincolnshire. Even by Phoebe's standards the illustration was complicated, and realizing this the artist had carefully added footnotes.

'Rachel' she had written on one side of the picture, and 'prizon' on the other. 'Do not xplane this to B G', she had added as an afterthought.

'She's put Rachel in her zoo,' guessed Naomi.

'Rachel's in it already,' Ruth pointed out, 'and what about "We have done it now"? She might mean anything!'

'Do not explain this to Big Grandma,' repeated Naomi. 'As

if anyone could!' There was a day of anxious waiting and then another letter arrived, this time from Rachel.

Dear Ruth and Naomi,

I hope you are having a nice time, I wish I was there too. Even for gastrick floo. Phoebe says she wrote and told you about me having to rob the post office. I never told anyone why but Im not going in again to buy stamps so I know you shouldnt post letters without but they get there anyway.

Love, Rachel

Ruth, who had been forced to part with nearly a whole week's pocket money to secure this masterpiece, groaned, and handed it to Naomi.

'Well, it's perfectly clear,' said Naomi, 'Rachel's robbed the Post Office so she doesn't want to go in and buy stamps, so she posted this without one and you had to pay eighty pence instead.'

'I can understand that bit,' answered Ruth. 'What I can't understand is how Rachel robbed the Post Office and what Phoebe's picture meant and who the prison was for.'

'I don't feel safe these days,' said Naomi. 'I wish we hadn't told them and then had to come away.'

'People who feel safe,' remarked Big Grandma, appearing from nowhere, 'are usually mistaken. Sorry to make you jump like that! You people are very tense this week, I've noticed!'

Dear Ruth and Naomi, (said a postcard from Mrs
    Conroy)
    *I do hope you are feeling better now. We will be
glad to have you back. Goodness knows what the
Little Ones have been up to lately, I'm afraid Rachel
has been very naughty but that's all over now. The
inevitable has happened and Phoebe has broken her
little train. Dad says see you on Sunday!*
    Love from both of us,
    Mum and Dad

'Poor old Phoebe!' said Ruth. 'They must have used her train
money for Joseck.'

'Must have done,' agreed Naomi, 'I wonder what Rachel's
been up to, and I'm worried about Toby and Emma. We'll
have missed three visits.'

'Write to them,' suggested Ruth.

Dear Toby and Emma,
    *We are nearly better now so we will be coming back as
soon as we can so do not get anyone else.*
    I hope you are well.
    Love, Naomi

Dear Girls, (came back a reply by return of post)
    *Don't you worry yourselves my dears your flowers are
all through fighting fit.*
    Toby

Lovely as springtime was in Cumbria, a feeling of urgency began to grow on Ruth and Naomi.

'A letter might arrive from Joseck,' worried Ruth. 'I never thought to tell those two to watch the post.'

'They might be telling anyone anything, at least Rachel might.'

'I've a feeling you'll be glad to go home,' said Big Grandma surprisingly on their last day.

'Not glad,' said Ruth, 'but we've got things we ought to do.'

'We love it here,' said Naomi, 'you know we do, but . . .'

'But . . .' said Big Grandma. 'Quite. Your faces are very revealing! Perhaps you'll tell me about it one day!'

'About what?' asked Ruth, but Big Grandma merely grinned at her and remarked that she was not so green as she was cabbage-looking.

'I wonder,' said Ruth on the train home, 'what Big Grandma knows.'

'About Joseck?' asked Naomi. 'How can she know anything? The trouble with Big Grandma is that she doesn't forget things. She notices everything and it goes into her head and makes patterns. Or something. So the more she notices, the more she knows.'

'Good job, then, that she lives so far away,' said Ruth heartlessly.

'Yes, lucky Mum's not like her!'

'Or Dad.'

'Phoebe's bad enough!'

'Phoebe!'

'Well, she thinks just like Big Grandma,' Naomi pointed out, and Ruth was silent, appalled at the thought of two Big Grandmas, or even worse, two Phoebes in the same family.

Mr Conroy was waiting for them as they drew into the home station; he nodded and smiled as the train pulled in, but couldn't wave because his hands were full of Rachel and Phoebe. He held them by the scruffs of their necks to prevent them from hurling themselves across the platform.

'Rachel's looking ready to burst,' commented Ruth.

Rachel was exploding with questions and secrets. Joseck and robbery conflicted with the excitement of Ruth and Naomi's return, and the desire to know what they had brought her, and how many people in Cumbria regretted her being left behind.

'Did anyone say they wished I was there?' she asked, peering hopefully into a carrier bag of spring cabbages and rhubarb from Big Grandma's garden. 'Has anyone given you anything to give to me? Did you get my letter?'

Phoebe asked no questions, watching detached and unruffled as Mr Conroy hugged the travellers and Rachel riffled through their luggage. However, as they left the platform, she remarked,

'Everything's all right in Africa.'

'Is it?' asked Ruth, immensely relieved. 'Everything?'

'Only in Africa,' said Phoebe, not wishing to raise her

sister's hopes too much. 'I told Big Grandma to tell you, when she telephoned this morning, but she said you'd already gone.'

'Gone where?'

'On to the train home, to here. She was ringing to say you caught it all right. I answered the phone. She said you were worried about something so I said to tell you everything was all right in Africa, but then she said you'd gone.'

'What else did she say?'

'Nothing,' said Phoebe, 'only, "Good old Phoebe".'

"We came home just in time!"

A letter from Joseck arrived the next morning, the letter that he had written describing the goats and the deer and the small cats in the hills.

'What sort of cats?' wondered Rachel. 'Lions? Lions are cats.'

'They're not small, though,' pointed out Ruth, but Rachel said perhaps Joseck was so used to living in Africa that lions seemed ordinary, like the squirrels in the park did to them. 'And small,' she concluded. 'I'll write and ask him. He's my friend too, now. It was my ten pounds.'

'What about me?' asked Phoebe. 'What about my train? I was going to send him my train money. I didn't know that Rachel had gone to rob the Post Office!'

'No one possibly could,' said Naomi. 'Only Rachel could think of anything so stupid. Or do something so stupid.'

'It was very brave of me,' said Rachel. 'You and Ruth couldn't think of anything except being sick.'

'There are books in the library on Africa,' Ruth changed

the subject. 'We could go after school and look up African animals. And he's our shared friend now, so we'll all write to him. He'll be glad to have four, I expect.'

The library was well stocked with books on Africa, and the girls had four tickets each, so they chose sixteen between them, which left a very large gap in the section.

That evening, in the gap when Mrs Conroy had gone to work and Mr Conroy had not yet come home, they composed a joint letter to Joseck.

'Let Naomi write it,' suggested Ruth who was cooking tea for everyone. 'She's the neatest.'

Dear Joseck,
*   Now there are four of us. Me and Ruth and Rachel*
and Phoebe who are our sisters. They are seven and . . .

'Nearly ten,' said Rachel.

'Nine and two months isn't nearly ten,' said Naomi, 'I'll put nine.'

'Ask how old Mari is,' said Ruth.

Seven and nine, wrote Naomi.

How old is Mari? Ruth wants to know. She cannot write because she is cooking . . .

'Beans on toast,' said Rachel happily, 'tell him that.'

She is cooking beans on toast. We have got sixteen books about Africa with pictures of deer and cats like you said. Kenya looks so beautiful. Rachel says do you ever see lions? In England it is spring, we have planted seeds and there are lambs where our Big Grandma lives. But no goats.

'Tell him Ruth is burning the bread,' suggested Phoebe, and Ruth dashed across the room and seized the blackened toast from under the grill.

Ruth is burning the bread, wrote Naomi obligingly, *Rachel is scraping the burnt bits off. It is strange to think this piece of paper is going all the way to Africa and you will read it.*

'Why did you put that?' asked Rachel.

'Because it is strange,' replied Naomi. 'I can hardly believe it.'

Love from Ruth and Naomi and Rachel and Phoebe.

A little baked bean juice got on to the paper as they all signed their names.

'Fancy our baked bean juice going to Africa!' said Rachel.

'Now what?' asked Rachel, having watched (from a safe distance) the ceremonial posting of Joseck's letter.

'Now get thinking,' said Naomi, 'because we've got to get more money.'

'There's still Phoebe's ten pounds. Where are you keeping it, Phoebe?

'In Mrs Collingwood's cage,' replied Phoebe, 'because she's the richest person I know. I thought she'd be the best at looking after it. You can still get Peter money, can't you?'

'Perhaps, but he might not last much longer,' said Ruth gloomily, remembering the scene she had witnessed only the day before. Mrs Collingwood had called her proudly into the kitchen as she returned from borrowing Josh.

'You'll appreciate this,' Mrs Collingwood had said, and Ruth had watched in horror as Peter, perfectly clean and civilized, had rammed toast soldiers into a boiled egg, consumed them with only minimal damage to his surroundings, and washed them down with gulps of milk.

'Fascinating, you've got to admit,' said Mrs Collingwood. 'Well worth going to Italy for. A kind waiter in the hotel trained him!' She disappeared to answer the phone, and Ruth, with great presence of mind, picked up the empty egg shell and showed Peter how to smash it flat on his tray.

'Good Peter!' she said, watching as with happy fists, he pounded it to fragments. She felt very guilty as Mrs Collingwood returned to the devastation, especially when Peter beamed at his mother because he had been good. She could see that nothing but the power of speech prevented him from explaining his new accomplishment. Still, she had Joseck and his school to think of; Peter could not be allowed to grow up too quickly.

'What else could I do?' she asked her sisters. 'Goodness knows what else that waiter taught him!'

'Peter likes smashing things up,' said Naomi. 'It's kindness really, to show him how. He'll never have such good chances when he's grown up. When are you going back?'

'Thursday after school. Mrs Collingwood said could I amuse him for a couple of hours while she cooks, because they're having a dinner party.'

'Perhaps,' said Naomi, 'it would be a good idea if every

time you went, you taught him something really aggravating to do.'

'No, I can't do that,' said Ruth. 'It wouldn't be fair. Anyway, he's learning to talk more every day, he might tell. I'll just not teach him anything useful, especially not English. Lucky that waiter only spoke Italian to him, so that's all he's learned!'

'Italian!'

'Oh yes, he says "hello" and "goodbye" and "thank you" in Italian now!'

'Teach him French,' said Naomi, inspired. 'That'll slow him down a bit, and it would be kind, too. I wish someone had taught me French before I knew any better!'

It proved to be a very good idea. Ruth, equipped with her French dictionary, spent an energetic and educational evening teaching Peter to count '*un, deux, trois*', while jumping off the sofa until he was completely breathless, after which they sat down and played Banging Books, a simple game, invented by Peter, during which Ruth opened all his picture books around him and he banged them shut again as loudly and quickly as he could. Ruth could open the books much faster than Peter could shut them, so she always won, but Peter did not seem to mind, and Mrs Collingwood was very grateful, announcing, with apparent satisfaction, that Ruth had obviously worn him out.

'How much did you get?' asked Rachel when she returned home.

'Two pounds.'

Rachel held a hand out for the coins and Ruth passed them over as meekly as if her little sister had a right to them.

'Naomi said I could look after the money,' explained Rachel, reaching down the front of her jumper and producing a small jam jar. 'I've already put our pocket money in. Much safer than the beastly Post Office!'

'What happens if you lose it?'

'Then Naomi will kill me,' said Rachel matter-of factly, having agreed that part of the arrangement earlier in the day. 'Is Peter civilized yet?'

'He's learnt to spit,' said Ruth happily.

'Good for you!' said Naomi.

'No, it wasn't me. It's another thing he learnt in Italy. They had to teach him because he kept eating the flowers off the tables.'

'You *can* eat pansies and nasturtiums,' said Rachel eagerly. 'Big Grandma told me one day last summer. Pansies are boring but nasturtiums are spicy. You could grow them in those old people's garden and sell them in bunches to vegetarians like Phoebe.'

'Don't be daft!'

'I could eat free sample bunches to prove it was possible.'

'It would just prove that you would eat anything; everyone knows that anyway.'

'And we could give Peter bunches of the wrong sorts, not pansies and nasturtiums and he could spit them out.'

'Rachel,' said Ruth, 'I'm not being horrible and I do think

101

it was brave of you to rob the Post Office, but I think you're crackers. Completely. Nuts. Right round the bend.'

'Food is food,' replied Rachel cheerfully, not at all distressed to hear these familiar opinions repeated, 'and we need money. Everyone knows you starve to death if you don't eat things, that's why they buy food. People pay money for much horribler things than pansies and nasturtiums!'

'School dinners,' remarked Phoebe.

'Well, anyway,' said Naomi, tired of the pointlessness of the discussion, 'we haven't got any pansies or nasturtiums. Or school dinners.'

Late in the night Phoebe awoke. A foot had trodden on her legs. A moment later another foot trod on her stomach, there was a thump, scurrying sounds and then a prolonged shaking of the bed as Rachel heaved her sledge up on to the top bunk and settled herself down around it. Phoebe knew the symptoms. Rachel was going to try to think and Phoebe closed her eyes and stuffed her head under her pillow in order to go to sleep as quickly as possible before she was called upon to help.

Carefully, Rachel tucked her sledge up with rather more than its fair share of the quilt, and then, comforted by its solid presence, began to order her thoughts. Scuffling through her mind she counted them out.

'Money. Food. Jam jar!' Yes, there it was, stuffed in a sock, wedged over beside eight of the sixteen books on Africa.

I really need a double bed, thought Rachel peevishly and wondered how much they cost. Pounds and pounds probably.

Suddenly a whole sentence of a thought came into Rachel's head all at once.

If I have any money, I spend it on food!

That was the clue she had been searching for, because not only did she, Rachel, spend her money on food, but so did all her friends. Money burnt holes in their pockets until they had converted it into nourishment and eaten it. All that was necessary in order to become rich, therefore, was to obtain food and sell it to her friends. But Naomi had said they hadn't any, not even pansies or nasturtiums. Rachel sighed heavily, curled up into the only shape possible between the books and the sledge, and fell asleep.

'Rachel!'

It was morning and Phoebe was kicking the underside of her mattress to awaken her.

'Rachel! I've thought of something!'

'Stop kicking.'

'Wake up! We've got to get up and make spare packed lunches!'

Rachel sat up, furious that Phoebe had produced so casually the idea she had struggled to grasp all night.

'Spare packed lunches!'

'To sell to people at school,' explained Phoebe proudly, 'you know, the ones who eat all theirs at break time and then have to beg for bits of other people's. Like you,' she added tactlessly.

There was a long, hurt silence from the top bunk while Rachel considered the advantages and disadvantages of accidentally-on-purpose dropping her sledge on to Phoebe's head and thus silencing her forever.

'Friday is a brilliant day to start,' continued Phoebe, unaware of the danger, 'because of Mum and Dad both having to be at work for eight o'clock. They never have time to think.'

That was true. That term, Friday had become the day that Mrs Conroy worked a morning shift at the hospital and the day that she was least likely to notice any unusual details of her daughters' behaviour. She would certainly never notice how many lunches they packed themselves in the morning.

'Have you gone back to sleep?' asked Phoebe, craning sideways out of bed to look up at Rachel. 'It's a brilliant idea, isn't it? It came to me all in a flash the second I woke up! But it won't be any good without you,' continued Phoebe. 'You always make the best packed lunches.'

Rachel, who had just balanced her weapon ready for the kill, granted Phoebe a reprieve and pulled it back again. After all, she *did* make the best packed lunches. It really *would* be no good at all without her.

'Come on then,' she said, and slithered out of bed.

Luck was with them that Friday morning.

'Fourteen peanut butter and banana sandwiches, twenty pence each, two pounds eighty,' Phoebe counted the takings at the end of the day.

'Three hard-boiled eggs, those ones I found in the back of the fridge,' said Rachel, 'that's another thirty pence.'

'Three pounds ten, then. What about the raisins?'

'Eighty pence. Eight handfuls, ten pence each, then the packet was empty.'

'We ought to charge more for raisins next time. Everybody wanted them. Anyway, that's three pounds ninety. Anything else?'

'That's all,' said Rachel, 'we ate everything else ourselves. Three pounds ninety is brilliant, though. Ruth and Naomi slave for hours for that much!'

'But we won't tell them yet,' said Phoebe.

'No,' said Rachel.

The difficulties began on Monday. Many were the complaints when lunch-time came round and Rachel and Phoebe's hungry class-mates, having confidently consumed their own lunches earlier in the day, arrived for further supplies and discovered that they did not exist.

'We didn't say we'd be doing it every day,' argued Rachel, chewing up her own packed lunch so fast she nearly choked.

'Just some days,' agreed Phoebe.

'Which ones, then?'

'We don't know yet. Fridays probably.'

'Not any other day?'

'Depends.'

'Well, what are we supposed to do now?'

'Don't know,' said Rachel, beginning her apple.

One particularly round and earnest child tried to reason with them.

'But I ate all my lunch on the way to school. Straight after breakfast, before nine o'clock. It isn't actually possible for me to survive until tea-time. I'll faint.'

'You won't,' said Phoebe unmoved. 'Rachel often eats her lunch on the way to school and she never faints.'

'But she's used to it,' persisted the Earnest One, and went away, unconsoled, even by the free gift of two mints and Rachel's apple core.

'We'll have to try and bring something tomorrow,' remarked Phoebe as they walked home that night. 'It's a waste of good customers, not having anything to sell them.'

'Yes it is,' said the Earnest One, who was dogging their footsteps, presumably in the hope that they would drop a crust of bread. 'I didn't faint but I feel very, very ill and weak!'

'Well, we'll bring something tomorrow,' promised Phoebe, thinking that he really did look ill and weak, and trying to remember what he had looked like in the past, before she had starved him.

'Definitely?'

'Definitely,' agreed Phoebe, despite her sister's dubious expression.

'We can't really promise,' said Rachel as the Earnest One left them and staggered feebly through his front gate.

'I'll think of something,' said Phoebe cheerfully, and the next morning produced from under her bed a sticky bag of marmalade sandwiches, constructed secretly in the middle of the night.

'They're all squidged up,' said Rachel, inspecting them critically.

'No one will care,' replied Phoebe airily. 'Look how hungry they all were yesterday!' The Earnest One reinforced her confidence by coming up to her with an anxious expression and informing her that he had eaten his lunch again and she'd better have brought something good.

'I have,' said Phoebe smugly. However, the Earnest One need not have worried. A rival company, the posh twins from Rachel's class, appeared at lunch-time with chicken paté sandwiches, cheese straws, chocolate biscuits, after dinner mints and a large bunch of grapes which they auctioned off to the highest bidder. It went to the Earnest One who consumed them with gusto and hoped that the twins would be there again tomorrow. Nobody bought any of Phoebe's sandwiches. She stuffed them in the back of her locker and went home, depressed.

'They *did* look rubbish,' said Rachel, not entirely sorry to see the collapse of Phoebe's idea.

'*You* needn't talk to me,' said Phoebe. 'You're a traitor! You bought those twins' sandwiches!'

'Only two!'

'Eating up the profits!'

'They were very good,' said Rachel unkindly, 'much nicer than squashed marmalade. I wonder what they'll bring tomorrow.'

Phoebe had been wondering the same thing, and so, apparently, had quite a few other people. Great disappointment was caused next day when the twins appeared empty-handed, very sheepish, muttering about their mother, and with school dinners booked for them until the end of term. Phoebe triumphantly retrieved her marmalade sandwiches from beneath her gym shoes, and disposed of her entire stock in minutes. The Earnest One, who had looked very frightened when the twins' business failed so abruptly, bought several sandwiches and was almost grovellingly grateful.

'What about tomorrow?' he asked. 'Thursday's our day off,' said Phoebe loftily, 'nothing till Friday now.'

'How much did we get today?' asked Rachel that night in bed.

'Two pounds forty, twelve marmalade sandwiches, twenty pence each, but that's without the sixty pence you gave to the twins, which makes it one pound eighty pence and three pounds ninety from last Friday. Five pounds seventy altogether.'

'It's a lovely way to get rich,' murmured Rachel drowsily, and fell asleep planning sandwich fillings for Friday.

'What have you got?'

That was the Earnest One, seconds after the bell had rung on Friday lunch-time.

'Crisp and tomato ketchup, peanut butter and tomato ketchup, golden syrup.'

The Earnest One sighed in delight and bought two of each.

'One pound twenty pence,' said Rachel, who was once again in charge of the money, as well as providing her own brilliant advertising by eating the sandwiches herself as rapidly as possible before they all sold.

'Any chicken paté or chocolate biscuits?' asked someone hopefully.

'Better ask the twins,' replied Phoebe.

That Friday was the beginning of Rachel and Phoebe's weeks of glory. Although there were some complaints (the unpredictability of quality caused problems, and not everyone could digest the fillings that Rachel invented from time to time) the service still remained popular. Rival companies, springing up with luxury fillings, tended to be so short-lived that they caused no real competition. 'Conroys' Homemade Spare Packed Lunches', wrote Rachel in her notebook. (She was collecting recipes in the hope of eventually having them published.)

'Do you think I really ought to call them homemade?' she asked Phoebe.

'Why not?'

'Well, you know where they're made nowadays. I just wondered if the publishers would mind.'

'I should think they would mind more if you called them dog kennel-made,' replied Phoebe, for recently, in order to avoid questions from their relations, she and Rachel had taken to constructing their sandwiches in Josh's kennel, a large and roomy apartment, easily accessible by climbing over the garden wall. There was plenty of room inside for Rachel, Phoebe, two plates, a loaf of bread, and whatever Rachel had decided should go in the sandwiches that day. Josh obligingly tidied up the crumbs for them afterwards. At first there had been remarks about dog hairs in the fillings, and several clients had disappeared for good, but Rachel and Phoebe had sworn earnestly that they were dog hairs from a very clean dog, and enough customers had remained to keep the business profitable – loyal, good-natured unspoilt people, who would eat anything gratefully, regardless of the fact that it was daily prepared in a dog kennel and stored in a boot locker. It was a happy time for Rachel and Phoebe. They grew very rich and began to talk of going to Africa, as soon as they had time away from the sandwich making.

Chapter Eight

'Saturday at last!' said Naomi, reaching over to shake Ruth awake. 'Let's go straight to Toby and Emma's.'

'What about Peter?'

'What about him?'

'I said we'd stop with him for an hour this morning, while Mrs Collingwood takes Martin to football.'

'*We'd* stop with him!' exclaimed Naomi. 'What a cheek!'

'I help you at Toby and Emma's.'

'Toby and Emma are different,' said Naomi. 'They don't scream. They're house-trained. They don't bite, they don't spit, they don't . . .'

'He'll be in the garden,' said Ruth. 'Perhaps he'll be better outside. Mr Collingwood's built him a playpen, huge, with high sides and a door that locks.'

'Sounds more like a cage,' remarked Naomi.

'It looks like a cage,' admitted Ruth frankly, 'a very posh one; they designed it specially to fit Peter. They measured his head and how far he could reach, so they knew how wide apart to put the bars and how high they had to make it.'

'They should have dug a moat round it,' said Naomi. 'All right, we'll do Toby and Emma this afternoon. What time are they caging up Peter?'

'Ten.'

At ten o'clock Peter was lifted into his play-pen. It stood in a sunny corner of the immaculate Collingwood lawn, filled with rugs, bouncy cushions, a rainbow collection of beautiful toys and several teddy bears. At two minutes past ten, Peter was hurling himself at the bars and roaring.

'How strong are they?' Naomi asked Mrs Collingwood apprehensively.

'Very,' replied Mrs Collingwood, leaning over the side to hug Peter. 'Very, very strong, my poor baby!' and she yelped as her poor baby sank his teeth into her shoulder.

'I'll be straight back,' she promised. 'I'm glad there's two of you!'

It took two of them to retrieve the missiles Peter hurled over the side at his departing mother's back. Josh came bouncing up to help too, but departed under a hail of wooden bricks.

'I'm not putting anything hard back in,' Naomi told Peter sternly, 'you're dangerous! Even Phoebe was never as bad as you!'

'He's not usually this awful,' Ruth said. 'I think we ought to just leave everything where he throws it and see what he does.'

They sat out of range while Peter emptied his playpen and then proceeded to tear up the lawn with his fists and teeth.

'He's getting awfully dirty,' remarked Naomi.

'I know, but he's stopped screaming and they're used to him getting dirty.'

'Ruining the grass as well.'

'Yes, Mr Collingwood said he would ruin the grass. It's only that one corner.'

'He's really strong,' commented Naomi, looking at the size of the clods Peter was excavating. 'What do they feed him on? Dynamite?'

'Martin said he was like that even when he only drank milk. Martin says he's quietened down a lot. He used to scream so loud he could hear him as far as the bus stop. And ringing in his ears all day at school afterwards!'

At that moment a fat hand shot out from underneath the play-pen.

'He's tunnelling out!' said Naomi in horror.

Ruth jumped to her feet and began picking up toys and putting them back into the play-pen to distract the captive. Peter, looking pleased, plugged up his hole with a plastic telephone and a large yellow duck.

'He just wanted something to play with,' said Ruth. 'He's being good now. Help me collect everything and we'll put it all back.'

Naomi obligingly joined the search for toys. Everything they handed to Peter he accepted with a large grin and piled into his corner. When he had a heap high enough, he clambered on to the top, hauled himself on his stomach on to the top bar and prepared to let himself drop. Ruth caught him just as he crashed to the ground.

'*Grazie*,' said Peter, and kissed her muddily on both cheeks.

'There,' said Ruth, flattered. 'He was lonely!'

'Yes,' agreed Naomi, and added after a moment's thought, 'you're going to have to go in with him!'

'In with him? In there?'

'Behind the bars,' said Naomi, and went home.

'It's a hard way to earn money,' said Ruth. Naomi was washing up the Saturday lunch dishes and Phoebe and Rachel were drying. By common consent, Ruth had been allowed to sit and watch.

'What did he do,' asked Naomi curiously, 'when you got in with him?'

'Nothing much. We played bears for a bit and then he fell asleep all in a heap and then Mrs Collingwood came home.'

'Was she cross when she saw him? What did she say?'

'Why would she be cross?' asked Rachel. 'Was Peter all covered in mud like Ruth when she came home?'

'Worse,' said Ruth. 'At least he looked worse, but I've noticed before that dirt shows up more on Peter than it does on most people.'

'More than on Rachel, even?' asked Phoebe, astonished.

'Maybe not,' Ruth admitted. 'Anyway, all she said was for me to bring my clothes straight round and she'd put them in the washing machine with Peter's before the stains dried in, and she gave me two pounds. And tea and chocolate cake and a bottle of posh bubble bath she'd had for a present and she said not to hesitate to borrow her books!'

'Not bad for less than an hour,' said Naomi. 'What sort of bubble bath?'

'Alpine strawberry and mallow.'

'You'll smell like a trifle.' Naomi emptied out the washing-up bowl and handed the last mug to Rachel, who dropped it.

'It's a waste to drop them *after* they've been washed,' Naomi told her reprovingly. 'You should smash them dirty, if you're going to.'

'It's only the handle,' Rachel inspected the mug, 'we can glue it on again. It's been glued before, anyway. Did you know we were coming with you this afternoon?'

'Oh no!' protested Ruth.

'Oh yes,' said Mrs Conroy coming in. 'Can't leave them alone in the house and I'm going shopping and your father's got to go back in to work. And I've sorted out some seedlings for your garden, Naomi, if you'd like to come and get them.'

'Free?' asked Naomi, following her mother to the shed.

'Since when did you hear of me charging old people for a few seedlings?' asked Mrs Conroy. 'A nice old couple like that, too; I dropped in for a word with them while you were at your Grandma's. You must be careful not to tire them out. I thought they both looked very frail.'

'Ill?' asked Naomi, alarmed.

'Just old,' replied her mother, who had looked at Toby and Emma with experienced eyes and decided that if they really wanted a garden and her daughters could do anything to help, then they should do it, and the sooner the better.

*

It was their first visit to Toby and Emma since they had arrived home. The garden that Ruth and Naomi had last seen a month ago, bare and wintery and sprouting nothing much but markers to show where they had planted seeds, had grown quite green and bushy in their absence. Someone (Mrs Reed, they later discovered) had cut the grass, but that was all that had been done. Weed and flower seedlings fought for space in the borders, dandelions lined the path, and the old apple tree, in full blossom, bent even lower over the garden shed.

'I can't get down to them myself,' Toby nodded at the weeds. 'You've come back just in time! And who are these two young ladies?' he asked, winking at Rachel and Phoebe.

'They're only Rachel and Phoebe,' explained Naomi, as she unloaded trays of seedlings and the sixteen library books on Africa from her and Ruth's bicycle baskets. 'We've got to look after them while Mum's out shopping. I hope you don't mind.'

'The more the merrier,' said Toby cheerfully.

'I can dig,' Rachel told him.

'You can that, if you've a mind to,' agreed Toby. 'Is that more books on gardening you've brought?'

'They're books on Africa,' said Phoebe. 'I needed something to read. You can look at them if you like. Have you ever been?'

'I have,' said Toby surprisingly, 'fifty-odd years ago! Hot and mucky it was!'

'What were you doing? On holiday?'

'Fighting.'

'You shouldn't fight,' Rachel told him primly.

'I don't any more,' said Toby. 'Now you make yourselves at home while I nip in and fetch Emma. She's been looking forward to you coming all day.'

Ruth and Naomi settled down to some much-needed weeding. Phoebe piled the library books into a heap, chose the most interesting, and sat down on the rest to read it. Rachel wandered around the garden, looking for a likely spot to dig for treasure.

Nearly an hour later, Phoebe looked up from her book. Ruth and Naomi had almost met in the middle of the long border. Across the lawn, Rachel had found a bare patch.

A humpy looking bit, thought Rachel hopefully. *Someone must have buried something here a long time ago!*

Someone had buried something there, and not so long ago either. Rachel, industriously scrabbling with her hands, gave a sudden screech of delight and came up with a red feather.

'Rachel!' Ruth and Naomi dashed across the garden.

'There's something under here!' Rachel announced. 'Quite big and hard, I can feel the edges! What are you doing?' For her sisters had seized the feather, shoved it back into the hole, and were piling in the earth as quickly as they could, all the while glancing guiltily at the house.

'You idiot!' said Ruth. 'Why did you choose that place to dig? That's where they buried Roger!'

Rachel looked suddenly very green and asked if Roger was another old man.

'Roger was their parrot,' Naomi said, 'and their last gardener got chucked out for digging him up!' Hastily she grabbed the box of geraniums and lobelias her mother had given them and began planting them over Roger's much-disturbed remains.

'I was only looking for treasure,' said Rachel, sniffing her parroty hands and giving them a perfunctory wipe on the grass.

Toby and Emma arrived just in time to hear her. 'No harm in looking,' said Toby. 'Where there's life there's hope!'

'What about where there's dead parrots?' asked Phoebe, but fortunately no one heard her.

'Don't you go digging too deep over there,' murmured Emma as she sank into the chair they brought her. 'I used to look for treasure when I was your age.'

'When you were a Guide?' asked Ruth.

'When I was a girl,' said Emma. 'I'll just get comfy,' and there was a pause of silence while Emma's bones and breathing settled into their new surroundings. 'When I was a girl,' she continued. 'You come over here and look at these pictures. These is some of the first Girl Guides!'

Curious, the girls came to look at the bundle of photographs Toby handed to Emma. A party of girls, long-skirted, wearing straw hats, looked back at them.

'Black and white,' said Rachel.

'Can you pick me out?' asked Emma.

In silence they stared at the group of round faces, tanned hands and arms, bright eyes and blowing hair.

'Are they all old ladies now?' asked Rachel, but before Emma could reply, Phoebe had planted a grubby, certain finger on to one of the hats.

'That's you!'

Involuntarily the girls glanced at Emma. More than eighty years had passed since the photograph had been taken, but even that did not seem time enough to wear any of those faces into one so old as Emma's, yet Phoebe said again, quite certainly,

'That's you! Anyone could tell!' and Toby and Emma were nodding in admiration.

It was the beginning of a strange understanding between Phoebe and Emma. It was a friendship of equals, both sides seeming oblivious to the eighty-five years that separated them. Phoebe made no concession to Emma's obvious frailty. If Emma fell asleep in the middle of a conversation, Phoebe did not hesitate to shake her awake again. She dragged Emma, willy-nilly, through her own convoluted ideas and theories, and when Emma did not understand, Phoebe drew pictures to demonstrate her thoughts, and explained the pictures to Emma. Emma retaliated by ignoring the fact that Phoebe was seven years old, completely poverty stricken, confined to school all day, and hampered by a family who all attempted to bring her up in different directions.

One summer Saturday they sat together in the doorway of the potting shed, under the apple tree, and argued.

'No good blaming other people,' said Emma. 'What's to stop you going? There's aeroplanes, isn't there? Flying over all the time!' and her head nodded suddenly forward.

Phoebe glared at Emma and poked her crossly awake.

'You need money. And passports. We'd never be allowed.'

'Flying all the time,' repeated Emma stubbornly. 'There's one now!' and she pointed to a white jet trail crossing the blue June sky.

'Full of rich grown-ups.'

'You don't know,' murmured Emma. 'I shouldn't let it stop me if I wanted to go!'

'Why don't you, then?'

'Don't want to,' replied Emma, 'garden's full of flowers!' and she fell so deeply asleep that Phoebe got up and marched away.

'Africa!' Emma's voice came scornfully through layers and layers of dreams.

Phoebe, who never told anyone anything, had told Emma all about Joseck. Toby knew quite a lot too; he must have heard from Emma. Strangely enough, the girls were not at all worried about this. Secrets seemed safe with Toby and Emma. They were no more likely to talk than the apple tree.

Sometimes Ruth worried about Phoebe's treatment of Emma.

'You shouldn't joggle her like that! It's rude and she's old!'

'It's rude to go to sleep when people are talking to you,' pointed out Phoebe. 'I don't joggle *hard*. Anyway, she wanted to be awake. She was choosing more people to put in my zoo.'

Emma had taken immediately to the idea of Phoebe's zoo, and had more or less enrolled as a sort of underkeeper. Phoebe had constructed a cage for her which she kept in the shed.

Lately, Phoebe and Emma had spent a great deal of time together in the shed, looking at library books about Africa and discussing their captives.

'What sort of people does she put in there?' asked Ruth curiously.

'Mostly dead ones,' said Phoebe. 'She doesn't draw pictures, though. She just writes their names on bits of paper and pushes them through the bars.'

Ruth knew better than to comment on this practice, and merely remarked, 'Well, don't wear her out, anyway. Come on, it's time to go home; Toby's paid Naomi.'

They met Naomi at the garden gate, looking far from happy. It had been very hard to take Toby's money that afternoon, especially as he had also given them chocolate bars and orangeade, a bag of apples and the parrot's old cage, in case they ever got a parrot. In the end, Naomi had settled for half the amount offered.

'What about yon lad in Africa?' Toby had asked, as Naomi dug her hands in her pockets and shook her head.

'We've plenty for him,' said Rachel cheerfully, and patted her stomach so that Toby could hear the jam jar rattle.

'Certain?'

'Oh yes,' said Naomi, although she was far from certain. 'Anyway, we only came to look at the garden and to see you. We've done hardly any work.'

'You've done more than you know,' said Toby. 'Ay well, we'll settle up one day.'

*

'What about Joseck, though?' asked Ruth as they walked home. 'We've only got six pounds and it ought to be posted by the weekend.'

Rachel and Phoebe glanced smugly at each other, and later that evening produced ten pounds in silver and coppers.

'We earned it,' said Phoebe casually.

'How?' demanded Naomi, and when they would not say, she glared very hard at Rachel and asked, 'Legally?'

'Oh yes!' said Rachel and Phoebe together, who honestly believed that it was legal to manufacture sandwiches out of stolen property in a dog kennel and then sell them to school children.

Ruth took the money very doubtfully, and purchased a ten pound postal order with some concern, although she could hardly believe that Rachel would have found the courage to rob the Post Office twice. It appeared that she had not; nothing happened when she went in, except that Rachel's cashier threw his hands up into the air and shouted that he surrendered, but then he did that every time a Conroy girl entered, so it was not unusual. Rachel's sisters were beginning to be extremely tired of the joke, but felt in no position to complain.

'We do need another way of getting money, though,' Naomi remarked that night.

'I know, I'm trying to think of one.'

Ruth fell asleep still trying, and it was not until her class trip to London that inspiration finally arrived. She came home exhausted, dirty, and glowing.

'Artists were drawing pictures, just in the streets,' she told Naomi, 'and people were giving them money! Paying!'

'In the streets?' asked Naomi, going cold with dread.

'*On* the streets,' said Ruth, 'on the paving stones! Chalks and pastels mostly. People stopped to look and put money in their tins or hats or chalk boxes!'

'Oh no!' said Naomi in horror. 'Anyway, it's begging!'

''Course it isn't!'

'I bet it's against the law.'

'They were doing it in London,' said Ruth fanatically, 'policemen everywhere. It can't be.'

'Anyway, I can't draw.'

'I can. And you could colour in.'

'I won't. It's a terrible idea. It's worse than robbing the Post Office. Someone might see us! Anything!'

'People are *meant* to see,' said Ruth, and Naomi recognised a familiar note of madness in her voice. Ruth, usually the sanest of them all, occasionally flipped. At such times she was not to be reasoned with; the only thing to do was to wait until the phase was over and then deal as best as possible with the consequences.

'I'm not colouring in,' said Naomi. 'I'm not doing anything to help. I'm not coming near you. I think you're mad. And you can do it in disguise, so that no one knows you're my sister!'

'Will you help me with the disguise?'

'All right,' said Naomi begrudgingly.

*

123

For the first time in her life, Naomi prayed for rain. She prayed that it would rain all summer, from the first day of the holidays to the last, excluding the two weeks they were to spend in Cumbria with Big Grandma. During the first week of the holidays, it seemed that her prayers would be answered. It poured and poured; the pavements streamed with water. It was the sort of weather to make any hopeful street artist search for an alternative career, but Naomi was disturbed to see that Ruth's ambitions remained undampened.

'It will wash the pavements clean,' she remarked, and went out into the down-pour to locate a suitable site for her efforts. Naomi refused to go with her and told Ruth quite frankly that she hoped she caught pneumonia, but Ruth returned home triumphant.

'There's a beautiful patch of clean paving stones right outside the church,' she announced. 'Just right, and miles away from the market and you know that's where all the policemen lurk about. We'll be quite safe.'

'What d'you mean, "we"?' demanded Naomi. 'You needn't think I'll be there, because I won't.'

'I think I'd better start practising pictures,' said Ruth.

'Where?'

'Guard the door!' said Ruth, and began rolling back their bedroom carpet.

'You're crazy,' said Naomi, but guarded the door while Ruth drew the local church, Van Gogh's 'Sunflowers' and Tigger from *Winnie the Pooh* on the bedroom floor-boards.

'Look at all the chalk you're using up!'

124

'I bought stacks,' replied Ruth. 'I spent all my pocket and Peter money.'

'What an awful waste!'

Ruth didn't bother to argue. The next day she rubbed out the sunflowers, church and Tigger, and drew a beautiful parrot and the Prime Minister's head and shoulders in black and white.

'Isn't it cheating to copy out of newspapers?' asked Naomi.

'They were doing it in London,' replied Ruth, not looking up and printing 'COUNTRY CRASHES!' very neatly under the picture of the Prime Minister.

'What'll you do if it rains all summer?' asked Naomi.

'The weather forecast says it'll be dry by the end of the week.'

Naomi looked very depressed and went on a mysterious trip to Toby and Emma's. She returned with a bulging carrier bag of old clothes.

'What's that?'

'Disguise,' said Naomi briefly.

A long letter from Joseck arrived. He wrote that he was well and very happy to have four friends in England. He told them that when he took their letter home, there was his mother, cooking beans and bread for supper, just like Ruth. He had read the letter to his family and his mother had laughed and said she did not burn the bread and his father said tell your friend Rachel that his friend saw two lions cross the road only a few evenings ago. He wrote that Mari was seven years old and made everybody laugh.

Then he wrote that from the school window he could see the bus from Nairobi coming along the road and that it had stopped outside the school and four people climbed out and Joseck had a thought that it might be his friends from England, although he knew all the time that really it was not.

Naomi sighed. Ten pounds a month were hard enough to find, never mind air fares to Nairobi.

'Have you and Phoebe got any more money?' she asked Rachel. 'We'll need to send another ten pounds before we go to Big Grandma's.'

Rachel and Phoebe shook their heads. The Homemade Spare Packed Lunch business had been temporarily closed when term ended.

'Ruth's going to get some,' said Phoebe. 'She told me she's found an easy way!'

'Easy!' snorted Naomi.

'Easier than looking after Peter, I think she meant. She wouldn't tell us what it was, though.'

Rachel remarked that she hated secrets and that she wished she knew what Ruth was planning and Naomi thought privately that Rachel was lucky. She wished she didn't know, and she wished it even more the next morning when Ruth's bed was found empty and Ruth herself could not be discovered anywhere.

'Well at least she had something to eat before she went out,' Mrs Conroy said, and she looked crossly at the crumbs all over the breadboard, the jammy butter and the bottle of spilt milk.

'Perhaps she got hungry in the night,' suggested Rachel, but Mrs Conroy said no, that was the morning's milk spilt all over the table. Certain clothes, an enormous straw hat and a greenish-greyish old mac of Emma's had disappeared from Naomi's supply of disguises. Naomi noted this fact with mingled horror and relief and told herself that it was none of her business.

Outside the church, in the early morning sunshine, the Owl and the Pussy Cat, Hey Diddle Diddle, the Prime Minister, a stained-glass window and Van Gogh's 'Sunflowers' already brightened the paving stones. A small shabby figure rested contentedly beside these glories, eating chalk, jam sandwiches and dirt in about equal quantities. Beside her, also eating a jam sandwich, stood the lanky figure of the vicar. He was admiring the design of the stained-glass window.

'It's the animals in the ark,' explained Ruth. 'I thought I'd do something religious because of the church.'

'Please don't get into trouble,' said the vicar.

'I've got old clothes on,' said Ruth cheerfully.

'I didn't mean that . . . Well, I shall be in and out of the church. Come and find me if you need to. Really I shouldn't encourage you, but good luck,' and the vicar dropped fifty pence on to the tigers in the ark and disappeared into the church.

For some time Ruth earned no more. People passing by the church on their way to the market square stopped to admire the pictures, but no one seemed to think they ought to pay for the privilege. After a while Ruth realized that they needed somewhere to put their money, and took off her hat. She started it off with the vicar's fifty pence and a couple of pennies of her own. Soon a steady trickle of money began to fall in it.

This worked until a small scruffy man in an old-fashioned hat and sunglasses walked very close to her, dropped a penny on to the picture of the cow jumping over the moon, and hissed, 'Put your hat on!'

He had such a familiar voice that Ruth looked up.

'Put your hat on!'

The little old man shuffled off, sat down on the churchyard wall and glared at Ruth. Despite the heat of the day, he wore a long overcoat and a scarf wound round his face, almost to his eyes. Wellington boots came up to the hem of his coat. Ruth was so sure that she knew who he was, that she left her pictures and sat down on the wall beside him. Immediately he leapt to his feet and hurried away.

At that moment a woman walked straight across the Prime Minister's face, said, 'Sorry, duck!' and dropped twenty pence into the straw hat. The vicar came out and asked, 'Everything all right? No trouble from anyone?' and by the time Ruth had retrieved her money and assured him that everything was fine, the little man from the church wall had gone away.

It seemed he had not gone far, however; he reappeared half an hour later and dropped a bar of nut chocolate on the man in the moon. Stuck into the wrapper was a note. 'Put your hat on. And your coat. Egg-Yolk Wendy and Gavin coming this way.'

'Naomi!' exclaimed Ruth and the little man nearly jumped out of his skin.

'Don't shout my name! And you're supposed to be in disguise! And rub that out!' Naomi pointed a wellington boot to where her sister had signed her name across the paving stones.

'Do you think it's too vain?' asked Ruth earnestly, and found she was suddenly talking to empty space. Naomi had leapt nimbly over the churchyard wall and been replaced by a very familiar pushchair.

'Good dog!' said a loud and friendly voice.

'Bad news!' announced Mrs Collingwood cheerfully. 'Awfully sorry but you're breaking the law, Ruth! Policeman approaching from the right! Vicar approaching from the church, peculiar little man hovering in the background! Time to stop, I'm afraid.'

Her voice was like sudden cold water on Ruth's dreaming head. All at once she awoke from the week's madness and saw the pavement of pictures, the policeman from the market threading his way towards her, the vicar hesitating on the path, and Mrs Collingwood's face. It bore the expression of exasperated cheerfulness that she usually reserved for late-night telephone calls from her clients at the police station. Ruth also noticed that Mrs Collingwood had thoughtfully parked Peter on the greater part of her signature, and was busy scuffing out the end she was standing on.

'Awfully silly to sign your name,' she remarked.

'That's what I said!' Naomi, hat even lower and scarf even higher, suddenly reappeared between them. 'Give me your money! Stuff it in this bag!'

'Good gracious!' said Mrs Collingwood.

'Quick, before that policeman gets here!'

It was almost too late. Even as Ruth transferred the last handful of change to the little man's bag, the policeman arrived beside her. Hastily the little man jumped the churchyard wall, dodged the vicar and sprinted across the gravestones. As he ran, he shed his hat and scarf, dropped his glasses and abandoned his coat. Before he was out of sight, he had transformed into Naomi, hurrying across the market place in wellington boots.

'That someone you know?' asked the policeman.

'Yes,' said Ruth.

Mrs Collingwood, to cheer Ruth up, informed her that she was the dirtiest person ever to enter her bath-tub.

'Impressive, you've got to admit,' she said, 'when you think of my husband after rugby, or Martin after football, or Peter!'

Ruth looked completely uncheered.

'Well, we can't go and talk to your mother with you looking like that! You know I had to promise I'd mention it to her. It all looked so odd; not just the pictures, but Naomi's clothes, and her running off like she did and the silly old vicar, offering to witness you'd been robbed!'

'S'pose he was only trying to help.'

'Lucky the policeman recognised me, and that poor old Peter was sick when he was! I wish I'd noticed him with that chalk. It may have been non-toxic, but it was a very nasty shade of blue!'

'Sorry.'

'I'll play it down to your mother,' said Mrs Collingwood reassuringly. 'Don't look so upset!'

Play it down as she might, Mrs Collingwood could not hide the fact that Ruth had been discovered drawing pictures in the street for money and had been ordered to desist from this rash enterprise by . . .

'A very pleasant man,' said Mrs Collingwood. 'I've dealt with him before. Very practical! A charming . . .'

'Policeman,' finished Mrs Conroy, who knew too well the pleasant practical men her neighbour usually dealt with. She was very angry with Ruth.

'So did she do it?' Rachel asked cheerfully that night.

'Who do what?'

'Ruth. Get that easy money for Joseck?'

There was a long silence while Naomi considered the day and Rachel gazed at her expectantly.

'Well, she got it,' said Naomi eventually, 'but it wasn't easy.'

CHAPTER NINE

The week before they were due to leave for Cumbria, the weather turned damp and dismal and the Conroy house seemed even smaller than usual. Smaller and full of suspicious glances. Mrs Conroy was keeping a close eye on her daughters, and no sooner did they disappear into their bedrooms in furtive twos and threes, than she routed them out again and found them jobs to do. Their reply to Joseck's letter was written in Toby and Emma's potting shed, the only private place they could find. Emma appeared in the doorway not long after they began. 'Saw you was here,' she remarked, sinking down on to the garden chair Ruth pushed towards her.

'Do you mind?'

'Why should I? What you doing?'

'Writing to Joseck in Africa.'

'Have you told him you'll be there one day?'

'We never could. It would cost hundreds of pounds.'

'In an aeroplane,' said Rachel. 'How do they stay up? What if it didn't? They don't give you parachutes. I asked Martin, and he told me.'

'Scared?' asked Emma, sounding surprised and shoving a new piece of paper through the bars of her zoo. 'I've never been scared of nothing. You put that in for me! My hands are shaking!'

Ruth took the slip of paper, and threaded it through the bars.

'Getting crowded,' she commented.

'Their problem,' said Emma. 'Anyway, I'm getting back. That was all I come for. You say hello to that boy for me.'

'I'm sorry,' Naomi inspected the envelope. 'I would but I've just licked it up and it's stuck. We will next time.'

'Say it when you get there,' said Emma, and she wandered back to the house.

'Get there!' said Naomi rather crossly. 'It's practically impossible even to get the ten pounds every month!'

'Mum's awfully mad with Ruth,' remarked Rachel.

'She's mad with all of us,' said Ruth. 'She hasn't got over you robbing the Post Office yet, or Phoebe smashing her train. It's not just me. I think we ought to try and not show up very much for a while.'

'What do you mean?'

'Just be there,' said Ruth, 'but not do anything that anyone would notice.'

'Slope around,' Naomi said.

'Unsuspiciously,' agreed Ruth.

'Not do anything?' asked Rachel, 'that's easy!'

For a day or two they tried this, and it *was* easy. Home grew peaceful and Mrs Conroy appeared to relax. It lasted until two days before they were to set off to Cumbria, and was spoilt by the Earnest One, who appeared on the doorstep, rang the bell, and asked Mrs Conroy if Rachel and Phoebe would still be doing it in the holidays.

'Because I think it would be a good thing,' he explained earnestly. 'People still get hungry! Even those marmalade ones would do if they did. I came to ask, in case they were and I hadn't heard.'

'What do you mean?' asked Mrs Conroy.

'I've been away,' explained the Earnest One, 'on holiday, so I might not have heard.'

'Heard what?'

'If Rachel and Phoebe still do them in the holidays. I know some people thought they ought to stop but I never did. They said it was a clean dog and it is, I've seen it. It's that one, isn't it?' and he pointed to Josh, who was enjoying the sun in the Collingwood front garden and looking, as the Earnest One truly remarked, beautifully clean.

'Tell me,' said Mrs Conroy, 'exactly what you are talking about. As if I were a very stupid person.'

'Are Rachel and Phoebe still selling those homemade spare packed lunches?' the Earnest One asked, as plainly as he could. 'The ones they used to make in that dog's kennel last term?'

'So much,' said Naomi sarcastically, 'for keeping a low profile and sloping around and not doing anything to be noticed!'

'Yes,' said Ruth.

'There's only me with any sense,' continued Naomi, conveniently forgetting that less than a week before, she had paraded through the market place dressed as an old man and had, thus disguised, robbed a street artist in front of a policeman, a solicitor and a vicar.

Ruth pointed this out to her, and Naomi said it didn't count because their mother had not found out.

'Only because Mrs Collingwood didn't tell on you like she did on me,' said Ruth. 'Anyway, arguing doesn't help.'

They sat together on the stairs and listened to the snivelling sounds that came from their little sisters' bedroom. Rachel and Phoebe had been cross-questioned and thoroughly told off.

'And you two can come down!' called Mrs Conroy up the stairs: 'Goodness knows, they need no encouragement from you! Do you realize what might have happened if anyone had been ill? Your father and I might have ended up in court! I've taken the money off them they said they'd made; what's left of it anyway. Six or seven pounds and apparently they've spent another ten on heaven knows what, sweets and rubbish I suppose . . .'

Ruth and Naomi cringed into opposite corners of the sofa.

'You'd think they weren't fed at home! First one thing and then another! The money that's left will have to go to charity, I suppose. I couldn't begin to try and give it back . . . I've told them if I hear one word about any sort of trouble at your grandma's, they won't be trusted to go there again. And the same goes for you two! Street artist indeed! I haven't forgotten!'

'They *were* doing it in London,' Ruth argued. 'No one minded there. It looked good fun!'

'Begging!' said Mrs Conroy. 'And that reminds me, you can bring down any money you got and it's going to charity, too!'

'There wasn't any,' said Ruth, 'not by the time I'd bought the chalks.'

'I'm speaking to your grandmother,' said Mrs Conroy, 'and warning her about everything that's happened this year, and if anything goes wrong, you'll be home on the next train!'

'What's worrying you?' asked Big Grandma. 'Have you been worrying non-stop since Easter, or does it come in waves? What have you all been up to? Strange tales have arrived from your mother! Is there anything you'd feel better telling me about?'

The long journey to Cumbria was over, the celebration tea was eaten, Graham, their friend of the previous summer, had departed for home. They sat together on the front steps of Big Grandma's house and watched the sun slide down towards the sparkling sea.

'Are you in trouble with the law?' asked Big Grandma cheerfully.

'Not now,' said Rachel, remembering with horror her run from the Post Office. No one else replied, so Big Grandma said no more until Ruth asked, as casually as she knew how, what people did to earn money in Cumbria.

'Farm mostly,' said Big Grandma, 'and tourism further inland, of course.'

'I meant children,' said Ruth.

'What sort of money are we talking about?' asked Big Grandma. 'Hundreds or thousands? Pounds or pence?'

'Ten pounds!' All four spoke at once and far too quickly.

The sun flamed brighter and brighter and Big Grandma, watching it, remarked, 'In Africa the sun sets at six o'clock every night! Did you know that?'

'Yes,' said Naomi, so abruptly that Big Grandma glanced at her.

'Of course, it will do on the equator,' Big Grandma agreed, 'obvious when you think about it, but I was astonished when I realized it myself. Everything still all right in Africa, Phoebe?'

'It'll be nice,' said Phoebe, after the shocked silence that followed this question, 'not to have to sleep in the bottom bunk, with Rachel and her sledge in the top one waiting to fall out.'

'You're always being horrible about my sledge,' said Rachel.

'Did you think of bringing it with you?' Big Grandma asked her politely, and Rachel replied that she had, and had in fact packed it in its sledge case in readiness, and had been quite prepared to carry it herself, but when she unloaded it at the station it had been taken from her by her mother.

'I'd polished it ready to come,' she said sadly.

'Life is hard,' said Big Grandma.

Ten pounds!

Big Grandma's granddaughters were in bed, and Big Grandma was thinking hard. Ten pounds was the amount she had given them each at Christmas, and the sum that Rachel had extracted in so reckless a manner from the Post Office. Ten pounds had been the amount Mrs Conroy had not been able to account for, from the funds of the Spare Packed Lunch Company. It seemed highly probable that ten pounds had been the amount that Ruth gained and lost in her brief career as a street artist, and it was more than likely that Ruth's Peter-sitting, and Naomi's gardening were done in order to obtain more ten-pound sums.

Big Grandma's brain fitted together further pieces of the jigsaw.

Strange that they were still obsessed with Africa. Big Grandma, helping with the unpacking that evening, had noticed that their holiday reading consisted of nothing but books on the continent. All these things, unconnected, had meant nothing reasonable to Mrs Conroy, but to Big Grandma, thoughtfully regarding Phoebe's sketch of the money inside her train through the slit, they were beginning to form a picture.

Ten pounds again, thought Big Grandma, *and obtained with disastrous results to the train!* Carefully she laid Phoebe's picture back down in the drawer of her desk kept for letters from her grandchildren.

'Extra pocket money! Holiday money! Call it what you like!' Big Grandma laid a ten pound note on the breakfast table. 'If it's the cost of a peaceful holiday it's cheap at the price!'

'Thank you!' said Ruth and Naomi together, amazed. Big

Grandma was smiling at her granddaughters as if she was fond of them, and although they realized that of course she *did* like them, she usually managed to conceal it so well that such proof was quite startling.

'Make it last,' said Big Grandma.

'It'll last us right till the end of September,' said Rachel and promptly doubled up with pain as three people kicked her under the table.

'Pigs!' said Rachel. 'Anyway, give it to me!' Reaching down into the stomach region of her sweatshirt she produced her jam jar, banked the money and stuffed it out of sight.

'Are you rich?' Phoebe asked Big Grandma. 'Where do you get it from?'

'Get what from?'

'Money. That ten pound note.'

'That particular one came from the Post Office,' said Big Grandma, grinning at Rachel, 'an institution which I hear you no longer patronize! Surely that jam jar is very uncomfortable?'

'Yes, very,' said Rachel, 'especially running.'

'Years since I ran anywhere,' mused Big Grandma, 'probably couldn't any more. Well, I'm glad you're pleased. You people worry too much! Stop it until September! Get outside and enjoy yourselves!'

In the middle of August the end of September seemed an age away. It was six weeks until they need start panicking about the October instalment of Joseck's money. Nothing happened to spoil that holiday; nothing bad enough to be reported to Mrs Conroy, anyway. They climbed the hills, made bonfires on the beach, picked blackberries and found mushrooms. Naomi discovered a pair of ancient sheep shears, and aided by Graham, who should have known better, sheared half of one of Graham's mother's pet lambs. The lamb, which had become quite a large sheep, escaped and took refuge in Graham's mother's kitchen.

'Thought you said it was a pet one,' said Naomi.

'It is, that's why it ran into the kitchen.'

'You didn't house-train it very well.'

Graham's mother, who had equipped Graham with a shovel and Naomi with a mop, explained that one could not house-train sheep, and Naomi, mopping round the cooker, privately thought that if that was the case it was silly to keep them as pets, but she didn't say so. She was very fond of Graham's mother.

'Lucky you have tiles,' she remarked as she sloshed busily around her hostess's feet, and Graham's mother agreed that it was.

Rachel did nothing alarming at all; she ate a lot, and what she could not manage during the day she took to bed and ate at night, but that was her own affair. She slept just as comfortably among the crumbs, egg shells and apple cores as she did in her own bed at home. Phoebe managed to fulfil a long-held ambition, starting Big Grandma's car and driving it unhurriedly into the forsythia bush. Fortunately, she neglected to take the hand-brake off, so it moved very slowly and no great damage was done. Big Grandma gallantly chose not to relate anything of it to Mrs Conroy, and they left for home with their reputations intact.

'How are you?' Graham's mother asked Big Grandma, meeting her the day after the girls had departed.

'Missing them, I'm afraid!' said Big Grandma.

Back at home, the girls missed Big Grandma. Despite her toughness and her sometimes unflatteringly honest opinions, she had always seemed to be somehow on their side.

'On the very first morning she gave us ten pounds!' Naomi told Toby and Emma.

'For yon lad in Africa?' asked Toby.

'She doesn't know anything about him.'

'Bet she does,' said Emma.

'Emma,' said Phoebe, remembering the conversation that first breakfast time in Cumbria, 'can you run?'

'Run?'

'Big Grandma said it was years since she'd run anywhere. Is it years since you have too?'

'May be. Dare say I still could though, if I wanted.'

'Go on, then.'

'Don't want to, do I? Why should I?'

'What if you wanted to run away from something?'

'I'm no coward,' said Emma, 'I told you that before!'

'No, and never was,' agreed Toby, watching Emma's head drop sleepily forward, 'and neither you be, either! You never get anywhere worth going by running away!'

'We don't run away!'

'You grab your chances,' said Toby. 'Like I did, when you come to see my garden. It's been a picture all summer!'

'Good,' said Rachel, who beyond digging up Roger, had done nothing at all to contribute to the brightness of Toby's garden.

'What's the plan for this afternoon, then?' he asked. 'We've a dozen cream buns wants eating when you're hungry. Would you like them now?'

'Big Grandma said if we cut the dead heads off things like cornflowers, they'd all flower again, so we thought we'd do that.'

'I'm going to dig for treasure,' Rachel told him. 'I haven't for ages.'

'Well, I can't say we've buried any since you last looked,' Toby remarked, 'however, no harm in trying. You're in the wrong spot altogether though; you want to be down by the marshes. That's where I used to look when I was a boy.'

'Why, what's down by the marshes?'

'King John's treasure,' Emma woke up as suddenly as she had fallen asleep. 'Have you never heard tell of that?'

They shook their heads.

'Every child in the district looked for King John's treasure in my day,' said Toby. 'King John, a bad man by all accounts, run off with the crown jewels and money and gold and goodness knows what. Dropped the lot crossing the marshes. That's history, that is; you should have learned it at school.'

'Why was he crossing the marshes?'

'To escape,' said Toby, 'though I don't recall what.'

142

'Why didn't he stop and pick it up again?'

'That's what I used to ask,' said Emma.

'How d'you know it's still there?'

'Because no one ever found it,' answered Toby reasonably.

'Be all muddy now, and rusty.'

'Jewels'll wash,' said Emma, 'and gold don't rust; that's what I used to think.'

Even Rachel was sceptical about the possibility of gold and money and the crown jewels lying round waiting to be found by some lucky schoolchild.

'How long ago was it?' she asked, 'because Ruth saw the crown jewels on her school trip to London before the end of term. Somebody must have found them and given them back.'

'There couldn't be two lots,' agreed Ruth doubtfully.

'I bet he picked them up again,' said Phoebe, 'even a really stuck-up king would bend down and pick them up again if he dropped the crown jewels! Even I would!'

'You're not a king,' Naomi pointed out.

'That proves it then,' said Phoebe dismissively. 'If I'd do it when they weren't even my jewels, then King John would definitely . . . there's Mrs Reed.'

Mrs Reed paused at the fence to admire the bright patchwork flower-beds, and called out, 'Bless you!' as she passed.

'Why'd she say that?' asked Naomi and Emma suspiciously.

'Oh, she says that every morning,' explained Phoebe, 'after school assembly, after she's read out what's banned. Last term she banned chewing gum, bubble gum, grass fights, running in the corridor, screaming competitions, talking Australian and my collection of ants I was taming in my desk. I expect she's just practising for school next week.'

'All them rules,' said Emma scathingly. 'You don't want to take no notice!'

'We don't,' said Phoebe reassuringly.

CHAPTER TEN

I n the second week of September, school began again. The
day before the beginning of term, Martin-the-good came
round and formally announced that he would no longer be
holding up the school bus for them in the mornings.

'But that means we'll miss it nearly every day!' said Ruth
astonished, and Martin said he was afraid that was the case
and he hoped they would not take it personally.

'What shall we do about waiting for the post?' Ruth asked
Naomi. 'Letters from Joseck might arrive any day!'

'We won't do anything,' replied Naomi calmly, 'and Martin
will hold up the bus for us just the same as usual. You wait and
see!' They were deliberately late the next morning, and sure
enough, there was Martin, one foot on the kerb and the other
on the bus, vowing he would never do it again.

'It shouldn't be allowed!' Egg-Yolk Wendy broke off a
detailed description of her summer to complain. 'Did you
know I've just come back from Europe?'

'No,' said Ruth shortly.

'Seven countries,' said Wendy, 'in two weeks! Eight counting England! Didn't Gavin tell you? I sent him a postcard and told him to pass it on.'

'Forgot,' mumbled Gavin. For once he was sitting on his own, Wendy's new sports equipment requiring all of the spare seat beside her.

'France, I was sick,' said Wendy, jabbing across the aisle at Gavin's foot with her new hockey stick, 'Switzerland, we bought four cuckoo clocks; Italy was all right except for the mountains and horrible toilets; Austria I quite liked; Luxembourg we just drove through, Dad said it wasn't worth stopping; Belgium really boring, then we had to go back to France though we'd seen it once already . . .'

Just to annoy her, Naomi moved and sat next to Gavin. Wendy tossed her egg-yolk yellow ponytail and said Naomi could if she liked because she was thinking of finishing with him and Gavin looked hopeful for the first time for months, but then grew gloomy again as Wendy added she intended to keep him for a friend.

'Who are you going to have instead?' enquired Ruth, and Wendy replied that she didn't know, but she was wondering about Martin who was so much more mature than Gavin. Martin laughed good-naturedly and said he would rather die and Gavin said, 'Oh please, Martin!' At which exchange of remarks, Wendy took offence and said she hated boys and wasn't going to be free at weekends any more anyway, because she was concentrating on sports this year: hockey, gymnastics and ice skating.

'Ice skating?' repeated Ruth, unable to hide her envy, and Wendy tossed her yellow ponytail and smirked.

'You'll be able to do what you like now on Saturdays,' Naomi said to Gavin.

'Will I?'

''Course you will! Didn't you hear? You won't have to go trailing round town after Wendy!'

'Won't I?'

'You've been dumped!'

'What can I do, then?'

'What did you use to do?'

It was so long since Gavin had done anything of his own free will, unorganized by Wendy, that it took him some time to remember.

'I used to go bird-watching down the marshes!' he announced, and was astonished to see Naomi's face brighten with interest.

Ever since their return from Cumbria, Naomi had been wondering about how they would find the next ten pounds. Gone were the days when she could bear to charge Toby and Emma for the work she did in their garden, and she had almost decided to choose the least-valued of her books and dispose of them in the town's second-hand book shop, when Gavin recalled his past life of freedom and awoke her imagination.

What if she were to find King John's treasure?

Her sisters, she knew, did not believe in it. Naomi had mentioned the subject again, and Phoebe had repeated her argument that anyone who dropped the crown jewels would certainly pick them up again. Rachel had agreed, and said they obviously had done, since Ruth had seen them in London only a few months before. Ruth had gone so far as to look King John up in the library encyclopaedia and had found no reference to lost jewels, or gold, or flights across the Lincolnshire marshes. On the other hand, Toby and Emma had been completely unmoved by what Emma called 'book talk' and had remarked that whoever wrote the encyclopaedia was obviously not a local chap.

'How do you know?' Ruth had asked, and Emma had replied that of course he wasn't, otherwise he would have put in about King John losing his treasure down by the marshes.

Anyway, Naomi decided, it was worth a try, and she asked Gavin, 'How did you get there?'

'Where?'

'Marshes.'

'On my bike,' said Gavin.

'Are you going on Saturday, then? Now Wendy's dumped you?'

'I only said I thought I would,' interrupted Wendy.

'Too late!' Ruth, Naomi, Martin and several other people who had pitied Gavin for months, all spoke together.

'I wish I could,' said Gavin, (uncomplainingly accepting the majority decision on his love life) 'but Dad's sold my bike.'

'You can borrow Ruth's,' offered Naomi immediately, 'if you'll show me the way.'

Gavin looked alarmed and said bravely that he didn't want any more girlfriends yet.

'No, no, no!' said Naomi through gritted teeth, 'I just want to go there, that's all.'

'You can't have got over me yet,' Wendy reminded Gavin, and Gavin meekly agreed that he hadn't.

'Good luck!' said Ruth the following Saturday. 'Hope it doesn't rain; it looks a bit grey! Don't let Gavin wreck my bike! I don't know how you got him to agree to go.'

'I didn't really,' admitted Naomi. 'In the end I just told him he was going and I was coming with him. I think he likes that better than having to make his mind up!'

It seemed Naomi was right. At every crossroads on the bike ride to the marshes, Gavin paused and asked Naomi which way she thought they ought to take, and each time Naomi replied with diminishing patience that she did not know and ordered Gavin to go the way he had always done in the past, and Gavin, following these instructions, finally brought them to their destination. With great relief Naomi abandoned him on a muddy patch of reeds and after impressing on him that he was not to go back without her, departed to look for gold.

The marsh was immense. It stretched out to the left as far as Naomi could see, and curved round to the right for miles. Far out on the horizon a silver line that was the sea marked the outward boundary. Naomi climbed a stile and squinted into the late September afternoon. Nothing Toby or Emma had said indicated the size of the place. She had imagined a large muddy field, and instead it was like finding another country.

'King John might have dropped that treasure anywhere,' she said. 'The fool!'

It was pointless even to get down from the stile. Naomi, hunched down against the cold sea wind, stared out into the greyness and searched for a glimpse of gold and at that moment the sun broke through the clouds.

Immediately the landscape was transformed. The munching brown cattle suddenly gleamed like golden beasts on an old tapestry and the bleached summer grasses acquired a blond rinse. Every puddle and pond and creek, right out to the glimmering horizon, became a sheet of mirrored gold. The crown jewels, stacked in a heap in the middle would have been impossible to pick out, and Naomi knew it. Eventually, stiff and chilled from sitting too long, she clambered down from the stile and went in search of Gavin. There he was, still parked beside his patch of reeds. He waved cheerfully as Naomi approached and pointed to a flock of birds that rose between them.

'What?' asked Naomi.

'Golden plover!' said Gavin.

Ruth was waiting at the gate when the treasure-hunters arrived home. The first thing she saw was Gavin's sad clown's face beaming with satisfaction and her heart gave a sudden bump of hope.

'Any luck?' she asked.

'Brilliant!' replied Gavin, causing her expectations to rise even higher, only to fall once again at the sight of Naomi. No hint of treasure sparkled in her sister's eyes. Her bike basket was perfectly empty, and her pockets completely flat.

'Didn't you find anything, then?' Ruth asked, disappointed.

'Golden plover,' said Gavin proudly.

'Golden what?'

'They're birds,' said Naomi, 'that's their name.'

'Oh,' said Ruth.

Tired and disconsolate, Naomi stumped indoors and up to her bedroom. No treasure at all! Even one small ring, or a single gold coin would have been enough, she reflected. She had not expected to come home completely empty-handed.

'Well, there's still Peter, I suppose,' said Ruth coming in. 'I said I'd look after him tomorrow morning while they go to Harvest Festival. And we thought of a way of getting money while you were gone, only it's a bit early in the year. Still, only a few weeks.'

'What is it?' asked Naomi suspiciously.

'Well, you know how people do Trick or Treat . . .'

'Oh no!' said Naomi.

'We could dress Rachel and Phoebe up in those old clothes you used for disguises.'

'You must be mad!'

'No one would know who they were, all dressed up!'

'They'd know who we were, though!'

'Oh well,' said Ruth, 'What about carol singing, then?'

'It's not even October yet!'

'The shops have had Christmas cards in for ages,' said Ruth earnestly, 'and anyway, we thought we needn't do carols straight

151

away, just ordinary hymns, and then get more and more carolly as it gets nearer Christmas . . .'

'It would be terrible,' said Naomi bluntly.

Rachel came in and announced that everyone was taking food to the church.

'Cooking apples and tins of beans and all sorts,' she said. 'Me and Phoebe've been watching them. What happens to it all after Harvest Festival?'

'What happens to church collections?' asked Phoebe, who had followed her. 'That's what I want to know!'

'Look,' said Naomi, firmly, 'I'll get the next ten pounds. Properly, without robbing the church collection or pinching the Harvest Festival stuff . . .'

'We only wondered about it,' Rachel interrupted, 'anyway, the church is locked!'

'How do you know?'

'I tried the door. Don't look at me like that! I only wanted to see all the food!'

'Oh yes?' said Naomi sceptically, 'and no one's going Trick or Treating or early carol singing either!'

'We didn't *want* to do those things,' Ruth said. 'I just thought we ought to. There's only pocket money and Peter left, and I'm worried about Peter. He's getting too many good habits!'

That was true. Ruth realized it again the next morning. Peter, who had spent the best part of two years scurrying round on his hands and knees with apparently no intention of ever walking upright, was staggering round the Collingwood kitchen.

'He'll soon forget crawling altogether,' said Mrs Collingwood complacently. 'He's getting to be a proper little man! Milk and biscuits for him on the sideboard, Ruth. See you in an hour or so. Kiss Mummy goodbye, Peter.'

Peter not only kissed her goodbye, but hugged Mr Collingwood too, and gravely offered his cheek to Martin. He further alarmed Ruth by waving sedately to his departing family from the window, instead of indulging in his usual practice of going purple and screaming.

Perhaps he's ill, thought Ruth, but not very hopefully, because Peter had never looked better. Or cleaner! It was amazing the difference walking instead of crawling made to his appearance. Gone were the grimy hands and knees and the red, breathless face. Instead he looked pink and white and very nearly human. He was beginning to show a faint resemblance to his brother, who was not called Martin-the-good by his neighbours for nothing. He was even beginning to grow hair! Real, shiny hair had begun to replace the worn, patchy fluff that had adorned his head for so long. It seemed the final blow. Ruth would have been less distressed to discover he was growing horns.

Naomi, who had been alarmed at her sister's hints about Peter and decided to inspect him for herself, arrived to find Ruth thoughtfully poking his head.

'What are you doing?' she asked. 'Has he got fleas or something?'

'Worse,' said Ruth. 'Look at him! He's growing blond curls! And walking on his legs and not screaming or smashing

153

things! He's been staring out of the window as good as good, waving to cars!'

'Why's he so clean?' asked Naomi, frowning at Peter's curls. 'He must have been up for hours.'

'It's because he's stopped crawling. Oh, Naomi, what are we going to do when Peter doesn't need babysitting any more?'

'I don't know. Can he talk yet?'

'No. Not really, only Good Dog and bits of Italian and French I've been teaching him. He can't say anything that makes sense.'

'Well,' said Naomi briskly, 'that's not so bad then! First we'll get him crawling again – we can teach him to play Omelette!'

Omelette was a game played by Ruth and Naomi in their extreme youth. All you needed was a sofa, strong clothes and a loud voice. Ruth had not known what an omelette was when she had invented the game; the word alone had fascinated her. She had crawled round and round the sofa, shouting it at the top of her voice until her palms and knees grew hot, and she was dizzy. It was a game that began in excitement, continued into frenzy, and ended in madness and exhaustion. Naomi had learnt it, Mrs Conroy had banned it, and since then, for years, they had forgotten its existence.

Now they looked thoughtfully at Peter, pulled the Collingwoods' beautiful green velvet sofa away from the wall, and began to play again. Peter watched them, startled but fascinated and then flung himself on to the floor to join in.

Never had Omelette been played so ferociously. Ruth and Naomi seemed to have lost the skill of crawling at great speed and dropped out after a few minutes, but Peter continued wildly circling, bellowing his chant of 'OmeletteOmeletteOmelette' until his knees gave way and he collapsed, sweaty and red-faced on Naomi's feet.

'Looks more like himself now,' said Naomi cheerfully. 'What next?'

'Milk and biscuits,' said Ruth, suddenly remembering and hurrying to fetch them.

Peter, hungry from his exercise, gobbled his biscuits as if he were starving and then got very milky down his front attempting to drink by lapping.

'Like Josh,' said Naomi, demonstrating.

'Good dog,' said Peter, rubbing his milky hands through his curls to dry them, and fell asleep in the corner of the sofa. Ruth, regarding him with pride, reflected that he would need bathing before lunchtime, but then the Peter she had known and loved in the past had always needed scrubbing several times a day.

'Oh my Peter!' exclaimed Mrs Collingwood, on seeing her offspring. 'What have you done to poor Ruth?'

'Nothing,' said Ruth hastily, 'he's been perfectly good! He didn't scream a bit when you left. Naomi came round and we played with him and then he had his milk and biscuits and went to sleep.'

'Well, it's sweet of you to spare my feelings,' said Mrs

Collingwood, still staring at Peter. 'Soap and hot water, I think! Say thank you to Ruth!'

'Grazie good dog,' said Peter absently.

'Practically a whole sentence,' said Mrs Collingwood, smiling proudly.

'Worked, didn't it?' remarked Naomi complacently when Ruth arrived home. 'How much? Got the jam jar, Rachel?'

Rachel fished up the jam jar and dropped the two pound coins Ruth gave her into it.

'If we put in half of everyone's pocket money this week and next week that'll make five. We need another five more.'

'I'll get it,' said Naomi.

CHAPTER ELEVEN

Dear friends Ruth and Naomi and Rachel and Phoebe,

I have been very well, and my family have been well. I hope you are well too. Thank you for the picture you sent with the letter. I was so happy to see you. All my family said, send our greetings to your friends, Joseck.

At school there is a board by the door with all the pictures of our sponsors. I have the best. I have the only children. Everybody says, Joseck has the best.

Mari said, 'tell them to come and visit. I need more girls to play with me. They can stay in my house.'

Then all the students shouted, 'No No They can stay in my house.'

I say you were my friends first. So you can stay at my house.

All the students in this school have had an injection. Now we will not have measles.

To be a doctor you must study at university. I should like to do that.

Your friend, Joseck

'Amazing to think,' said Ruth, 'that we have somewhere to stay in Africa!'

'Lots of places to stay,' added Rachel.

'You have to be very brainy to be a doctor,' said Naomi thoughtfully.

'Joseck is very brainy.'

'I know.'

Toby, who had listened with interest to Joseck's letter said, 'A doctor, eh, Emma? What about that?'

'Good lad,' said Emma, nodding slowly. 'Good lad. Good girls. All them bright flowers,' and then fell so deeply asleep that even Phoebe could not shake her awake.

'Leave her be,' said Toby gently, 'she got tired today, sitting out in your garden. Anyway,, she's said what she wanted to say.'

Rachel and Phoebe went outside to play zoos in the shed. Ruth tiptoed across to the kitchen to make a cup of tea for Toby. Naomi reread the letter.

A doctor! she thought, and *Gosh!*

The notice in the shop window read: BOOKS BOUGHT AND SOLD. Naomi paused to reread it before pushing open the door and marching in. She carried two large bags of books from the bookshelves of herself and her sisters.

The shop seemed at first to be empty, but at the thump of Naomi's bags on the floor, a door at the back creaked, and the owner appeared. Naomi was pleased to see that he was thin and bald and looked as nervous as she felt.

'Books bought and sold,' she quoted bravely. 'I've brought some books.'

'To sell?' asked the owner.

'It says that you buy books in the window. What sort of books? Old ones?'

'All sorts. The older the better.'

'Some of mine are very old,' said Naomi, relieved. 'What about children's books?'

'Very collectable these days.'

'Well, mine are mostly children's ones,' said Naomi, feeling more and more confident, 'that me and my sisters have collected.'

'And now you want to sell them?'

'That's why I've brought them.'

'And your sisters want to sell them too?'

Naomi looked uncomfortable, but reflected that if her sisters did not exactly want to sell them, they certainly wanted the money they would bring.

'We couldn't all come,' she said evasively, and began unpacking her bags on to the counter. The first to come out were four Bibles that she had stuffed in at the last minute.

'They *look* new,' she said anxiously, watching the bookshop owner pick them up, 'but only because we never read them. They're old, really. They were christening presents. You can tell by the dates.'

'Ruth, Naomi, Rachel and Phoebe Conroy,' read the bookshop owner, studying the dates, 'and you are?'

'Naomi. These are really old! That's why the covers have come off.'

'Paperbacks.'

'Yes, and these are old too.'

'School books.'

'Not pinched from school,' Naomi reassured him. 'They were throwing them out last term. These were Mum's, so they're very, very old!'

'Annuals.' The bookshop owner brightened up and began examining the dates, 'Any more?'

'These are Sunday school prizes that were Grandma's. They look quite new, but they're really ancient. Only they're full of stories with morals so we never bother with them. Someone might, though.'

'Someone might, certainly,' agreed the bookshop owner. 'Anything more?'

Naomi shook her head and looked anxiously at the pile of books on the counter. 'How much will I get?'

'How much were you thinking of ?'

'For all of them?'

'Certainly. The annuals and the Sunday school prizes, anyway. I can dispose of the rest if you like.'

Naomi sighed with relief and said she wanted as much as possible, preferably twenty-five pounds and the bookshop owner shook his head and said he thought not, and offered five.

'Twenty,' said Naomi.

'Sorry, my dear.'

'Fifteen?'

'How about ten?' suggested the bookshop owner, 'which is as much as you'll get anywhere.'

'Ten,' said Naomi. 'Oh well, ten'll do. Can I have it now?'

'I shall just need your telephone number,' the bookshop owner grew suddenly brisk. 'Will your mother be at home? Or your father?'

'What for?' asked Naomi, very alarmed to see that he had already pulled a telephone directory from under the counter and was turning up the Cs.

'Always check with parents before buying off children,' he murmured, running his finger down the list. 'First rule of business! Good heavens!'

Naomi, horrified, had grabbed her books off the counter, stuffed them back into her bags, yanked open the door and disappeared.

'Good heavens!' repeated the bookshop owner again. 'No more than I guessed, though!' and he gazed regretfully for a minute out of the window. It was a pity about the annuals, he thought.

Peter, very dirty around the knees from playing Omelette, sat in his high chair and ate his egg as beautifully as he had been taught by the Italian waiter. Having finished it, he seized the shell, turned it upside-down and pounded it flat on his tray.

'Good dog?' he asked, looking at his mother out of the corner of his eye.

'Bad dog!' said Mrs Collingwood. 'Sorry, darling! I mean

161

Bad Peter! You didn't learn to do that in Italy! Or anywhere else, for that matter! Naughty Peter! Drink your milk!'

'Woof did,' remarked Peter, wiping eggshell into his hair.

Mrs Collingwood looked at him in amazement. 'I'm sure she didn't, if you said what I think you said!'

'Woof *did*,' Peter told himself quietly, reaching for his milk and sticking his tongue in it like Josh did. 'Woof did! Woof did!' and he sneezed very hard into his mug.

'*That's* not the way to drink!' said Mrs Collingwood. 'Really, Peter! What a mess! You've never done that before!'

Peter looked up with the expression of one determined to see justice done.

'Nayo does!' he said, and bent to try and lap out of his mug again.

'Peter!' exclaimed Mrs Collingwood, just managing to seize it as it tipped.

'Nayo,' said Peter firmly, 'does!'

Mrs Collingwood said nothing, but looked at him very oddly as she unstrapped him and dumped him on the floor. He dropped to his knees immediately and started playing Omelette round and round the kitchen table.

'Peter,' said Mrs Collingwood, 'that is a horrid, noisy game. Who plays it with you? Martin? Nursery?'

'Omelette, omelette, omelette!' shouted Peter. 'Woof and Nayo play! Woof!'

'Yes,' said Mrs Collingwood.

'And Nayo!' said Peter triumphantly.

*

Naomi ran and ran, her breath coming in painful jerks, the heavy bags of books knocking her shins. When she had given in to the impulse to sell their christening presents, she had forgotten all about their names being inside. Now her only hope was to reach home before the bookshop owner could telephone her parents. Perhaps she could answer the phone herself and, disguising her voice, deny all knowledge of Naomi Conroy.

I've done this before, she realised, remembering the run from Ruth's pavement artist adventure, and she forced herself to slow down to a walk as she came up to the church. At the gate the vicar stood, talking to a party of visitors, and Naomi hoped she would not be recognised as the shabby little man who had robbed her sister only a few weeks before. Strange to see those paving stones bare again! Naomi, walking as quickly and inconspicuously as possible, had a sudden mental image of herself, the dark little man, haunting that spot a hundred years into the future, while Ruth, a shadowy, kneeling ghost, perpetually chalked vanishing pictures on to the pavement.

'Hey, Naomi! Wake up!' called a familiar voice, and Naomi looked up to see Gavin grinning down at her from a shining new bike and looking most un-Gavinishly cheerful.

'Nearly ran you over!' said Gavin.

'I'm in an awful rush.'

'I'll walk with you a bit. I'd take your bags only my carrier's full already!' Gavin proudly indicated an enormous bulging heap of flasks, rugs, binoculars, waterproofs and wellington boots, all strapped into a bundle on to the back of his bike.

'Going bird-watching,' he said casually.

Naomi thought it looked more like he was going round the world, and would have said so, if she'd had breath enough to speak.

'Guess how I got the bike,' said Gavin.

'Birthday?'

'No. Congratulations present from Dad for dumping Wendy! Anyway, see you!' and he rode off before Naomi could begin to reply

Wendy dumped him! she thought, slightly resentfully, as she began to run again, and she thought how strange it was to feel sorry for Egg-Yolk Wendy.

Above her head the church clock struck three. How long had it been since she left the bookshop, she wondered? More than ten minutes? Time for him to have found her telephone number yet? Nothing to do but carry on running, while all the time her hands grew more sore and numb from the bumping bags of books.

Nearly home. Past Rachel and Phoebe's school, and the Earnest One's house, where the Earnest One was actually swinging on the gate. He peered eagerly into Naomi's bags as she passed and asked, 'Where's Rachel and Phoebe?'

'Probably eating enormous sandwiches somewhere,' replied Naomi cruelly, and hurried on.

'Wait for me!'

Naomi turned crossly and saw that he had left his gate and was panting after her.

'Can I come home with you?'

'No you can't! What for?'

'A sandwich?' he said hopefully.

'No you definitely can't! No wonder you're s . . .'

Naomi stopped, just in time.

'What?' he demanded suspiciously.

'Such a bother,' said Naomi, and to shake him off she dashed into the Post Office and then out again as the counter staff all burst into laughter and threw their hands up in the air.

Tottering with exhaustion, Naomi jogged slowly past the Collingwoods' house, arrived thankfully at her own, and came to a sudden, dismayed halt.

Something was happening. Mrs Collingwood was in the front garden, talking earnestly to Ruth, who was looking uncomfortable. Their mother was listening with a very grim expression on her face. From the Conroys' open front door came the sudden sound of the telephone ringing, and Mrs Conroy disappeared inside to answer it.

'Nayo!' cried Peter, suddenly catching sight of his friend and bouncing with delight. Naomi, after one startled glance, turned and fled, pursued by cries of 'Nayo! Nayo! Nayo!' faint and plaintive, hunting her through the streets.

Confused and horrible thoughts pounded through Naomi's head as she struggled along. The bookshop owner had found her number and telephoned her mother, and she had been seen, caught red-handed with her arms full of evidence. No chance of slipping in quietly now. Ruth was in trouble, that was clear, and Peter had learned to talk! It was impossible not to imagine that the facts were unconnected. What on earth should she do with these horrible books? And, for that matter, what on earth should she do with herself?

All at once, the solution came to her. She would go to Toby and Emma's and leave the books in their garden shed, and then she would go to the bungalow and sit in their quiet, bare room and do nothing. Rest. Not even think. And Toby and Emma, with whom no secrets were necessary, would let her.

With the exhausted, peaceful feeling of waking from a nightmare, Naomi wandered through the streets to where Toby and Emma lived.

'We ought to cut the grass,' she said to herself as she came within sight of the bungalow. The lawn was beginning to look ragged and shaggy, scattered with fallen leaves. Autumn had arrived in the garden. The borders, although still bright with flowers, had a tumbled, tangled look. Recent winds had brought small, yellow apples down from the apple tree and they littered the ground and path.

'I'll pick them up before I go in,' decided Naomi, pleased to think of one useful thing she could manage that day. It was strange not to find Emma in the garden. Lately, she had spent every bright afternoon nodding by the flower-beds, tucked up in layers of rugs and blankets against the chilly wind.

Naomi glanced across at the windows to see if anyone was looking out. Nobody was there, but the front door opened and Mrs Reed appeared. It was only then that Naomi noticed the cars parked outside the fence.

'Have they got visitors?' she asked Mrs Reed, surprised.

Mrs Reed, catching sight of Naomi for the first time, stared at her in concern. 'Yes, visitors,' she agreed after a moment. 'Shouldn't you be at home?'

'Why?' asked Naomi. "It's Saturday! We always come and see them at the weekend but if they've got people there, I'll just leave these bags in the shed.'

Mrs Reed, however, seemed to think otherwise, and with a hand on Naomi's back, she steered her away from Toby and Emma's gate. Naomi tried to wriggle away, but Mrs Reed, a headmistress, was an expert at steering unwilling people. Over the years, with that firm hand between the shoulders, she had steered hundreds of reluctant people in directions they did not wish to take: sinners to teachers' desks to confess, the unwashed to cloakrooms, heroes and heroines on to public stages to receive prizes, sworn enemies to make up with each other. Now she steered Naomi to her car, opened the door, took possession of the bags of books and stowed them, together with her outraged and ungrateful passenger, into the front seat.

'I'll drop you off at home,' she said. 'I need to see your mother.'

Another person complaining, thought Naomi, alarmed, and glanced at Mrs Reed apprehensively.

She did not look angry; tired and worried, perhaps, but kindly.

'I don't want to go home yet,' Naomi told her. 'I really wanted to leave these things in the shed. I could have easily waited there until their visitors were gone. I wanted to get the apples picked up, too; they've fallen all over the path.'

Mrs Reed did not answer for a minute, and when she did all she would say was, 'Don't worry about the apples, Naomi.'

Naomi, subsiding sulkily into her seat, wondered what awaited her at home. As the car pulled up outside the Conroys' gate, she was relieved to see that there was no one in the garden. Mrs Collingwood and Peter had disappeared, but Ruth stood at their bedroom window, staring out into the street, looking unhappy and mutinous. She jumped as she saw Mrs Reed and Naomi climb out of the car, and then, as Mrs Reed hurried ahead to the front door, she caught Naomi's eye, pointed firmly at herself and then her sister, and drew a horizontal line across her throat with her finger.

Both of us in trouble, then, thought Naomi, as she sidled in behind Mrs Reed.

'Mrs Reed!' exclaimed Naomi's mother, answering the front door, and then, catching sight of her daughter skulking in the background, 'Naomi!' in a tone that bode no good at all for Naomi. She got no further, however. Mrs Reed laid a gentle hand on Mrs Conroy's arm, shook her head slightly and asked if she might have a quick word. Naomi seized the opportunity to escape upstairs to Ruth.

'You got away quickly!' said Ruth, as she opened the door. 'Mum's planning to kill you, when she's done me! What did Mrs Reed want? Are Rachel and Phoebe in trouble too?'

Naomi dropped the bags of books with a sigh of relief. 'Feels like I've been carrying them for years,' she remarked, kicking them under her bed. 'I don't know the answers to any of your questions,' and she flopped down wearily on to her quilt.

'A man from a bookshop rang up about you!' Rachel and Phoebe burst into the room. 'What's Mrs Reed doing here?'

'She's probably come about you,' said Ruth. 'What have you done?'

'Nothing at all,' said Phoebe.

'Lately,' said Rachel, 'I don't think. It's getting hard to remember everything people say we've done wrong. Do you want to know what the man from the bookshop said about you?'

'No.' Naomi rolled over on to her back and closed her eyes.

'Well, don't you want to know what Peter went and said?'

'No. I don't care. I've given up caring!'

'What about?'

'Everything,' said Naomi dreamily. 'It's a lovely feeling!'

Ruth, Rachel and Phoebe stared at her crossly. They had no intention of leaving her to wallow in lovely, non-caring feelings while they suffered with their consciences.

'The man from the bookshop said you were trying to sell books that didn't seem to belong to you!'

'They didn't,' agreed Naomi placidly, 'so he was right. They were mostly yours, actually.'

'And he said you ran off very guiltily. He hoped you got home all right. Mum said she'd send you round to apologize for wasting his time. She's furious!'

'Poor Mum,' said Naomi, still with her eyes shut.

'And Peter's told Mrs Collingwood we taught him to play

Omelette. And that I showed him how to bash up his egg shells and you showed him how to lap up milk, like a dog. And Mrs Collingwood said she wasn't angry . . .'

'Well then,' said Naomi, 'what's it matter?'

'But very puzzled. And Mum said we weren't to be trusted.'

'Well, I s'pose she's right,' agreed Naomi.

'Don't you care what happens to us?'

'No.'

'Do you know why Mrs Reed is here?' asked Rachel, who had been very quiet, trying to work out which of her many recent sins might have come to her headmistress's attention. 'I don't suppose you care about that, either!'

'Not a bit,' agreed Naomi, cheerfully.

'How are we going to get Joseck's money? Or don't you care?'

'I don't know. Someone else will have to think of something. I've run out of ideas.'

'Where did Mrs Reed grab you?'

'Toby and Emma's.'

'I thought we might go tomorrow,' said Ruth. 'Are they all right?'

Naomi opened her eyes and sat up, suddenly remembering something she did still care about.

'I don't know. I didn't see them. Mrs Reed grabbed me at the gate and I couldn't get away. There were cars outside and she said they had visitors.'

'They couldn't have,' said Phoebe, 'they never do. Emma

says she can't be bothered with people who treat her like she's old . . .'

At that moment the bedroom door was pushed open and Mrs Reed came in, followed by Mrs Conroy.

'Treat who like she's old?' asked Mrs Reed, sitting down on Naomi's bed.

'Emma.' Phoebe stared at her headmistress in astonishment. 'But we never do. Why?'

'I just wondered who you were talking about,' said Mrs Reed, 'I'm sure you never did. That's why she loved having you there so much.'

Startled by something they could not name, Ruth and Naomi glanced at each other and then at their mother. For the first time they noticed her eyes.

'Emma died this morning,' said Mrs Conroy, and all the jigsaw puzzle pieces of Naomi's afternoon fell slowly into place.

CHAPTER TWELVE

T he Conroy girls were in disgrace. It was not the familiar shabby state of disgrace in which one or another of them had spent so much of the spring and summer, and from which they might soon emerge, forgotten, forgiven and reinstated into family life. This was bad, awful, dire disgrace. Their mother was ashamed of them. She felt she could neither help or understand her daughters. She treated them with furious bewilderment.

This had been going on ever since she and Mrs Reed waited anxiously in Ruth and Naomi's bedroom for the reaction to the news of Emma's death.

'Emma dead?' exclaimed Ruth in dismay. Her thoughts flew wildly. Emma! Toby and Emma and planting the garden. For weeks now they'd done it entirely for love. They'd begun it for money, but they hadn't let Toby pay them for ages.

'Emma . . . oh no!' Ten pounds a month was never far from Ruth's worries, and that's why she said, hardly knowing she'd said it. 'I suppose it won't make any difference!'

Poor Mrs Conroy was utterly shocked.

Then Naomi made everything very much worse by pulling her pillow over her head and saying she just didn't care.

'I don't care,' repeated Naomi, 'I don't care, I don't care. I've stopped caring about everything!'

Phoebe remarked cheerfully, 'It's not true and I don't believe it!'

No amount of explanations had been able to convince her. The only tears shed that afternoon had been by Rachel; and she, on closer inspection, was found to be crying over a jam jar of money.

'Things will get better.' Mr Conroy repeated this hope over and over again to his wife. 'They're good girls. It's shock. Things will get better, you'll see.'

As far as Mrs Conroy could see, they got worse.

'You'd think there'd be tears,' she said. She had been proud of the girls, and the way they had worked to make the bright, shabby, patchwork garden. She wept herself now, for Ruth and Naomi's blank-faced calm, as much as for Toby and Emma.

Mr Conroy understood a little. 'Beyond tears,' he suggested and he was right.

For the first few hours they were beyond tears. Except for Phoebe, they were so unhappy it ached like a strong dull pain. It was bigger than they were and they didn't know how to deal with it. After their mother and Mrs Reed had left them alone, they lay on their beds, curled up like hedgehogs, all prickles and darkness and fear.

It was Ruth who uncurled first.

'Look,' she said, late on Saturday night, 'we're not doing any good like this. We ought to go straight down to see poor Toby. It's too late now, but we could go tomorrow.'

On Sunday, however, Mrs Conroy flatly refused to let them out of the house. Ruth and Naomi didn't argue, but the next morning they missed the bus for school.

'If there's someone there already, we'll come away,' said Naomi, 'or if he looks like he wants to be on his own.'

But there was no one there, and Toby, who seemed to have been expecting them, showed no signs of wanting to be alone.

'Tell us when you want us to go,' said Ruth. 'We thought you might be lonely.'

'What about school?' asked Toby.

'Blow school,' said Naomi briefly.

'Ay well, it does get like that sometimes,' Toby agreed, and said no more on the subject. He seemed so pleased to have someone to talk to, that Ruth and Naomi stayed until their usual time for leaving school, returned home, and repeated the performance for the next two days.

'But we can't do it for much longer,' said Ruth, worriedly. 'We ought to be earning money.'

'How?' asked Naomi bleakly. 'Babysitting was the last way we had, and now Peter's ruined it. I couldn't sell the books. There's no one to ask. We'll have to give up.'

'No.'

'What then?'

Ruth's mind went round and round. 'If . . . if . . . we sold things at school.'

'Packed lunches?' asked Naomi, bitterly. 'That didn't work.'

'Homework answers! If we did people's homework . . .'

'Oh Ruth! We don't do our own!'

'If we asked for school dinners instead of packed lunches, and kept the money instead?'

Naomi groaned.

'If we could borrow it from Mum without telling her. Or Dad.'

'No,' said Naomi.

'No. I know.'

It was hopeless.

They were not the only ones miserable. Rachel had started sleeping with her sledge again. Phoebe, after having totally ignored the subject for two days, marched up to Naomi one night and demanded, 'Is Emma really dead?'

'You know she is,' Naomi told her, and she had not replied, but later on Mrs Conroy had noticed a change in Phoebe's zoo. The inmates who had languished there for so many months had all been released. Instead, every cage was littered with slips of paper. Emma's name was on all of them.

'Why, Phoebe?' Mrs Conroy had asked.

'Because she's dead,' said Phoebe, furious, but unable to find the words to explain that as far as she was concerned Emma had deserted her, left her friend to cope alone, vanished in the middle of an argument, died without a word of explanation or farewell.

Phoebe, with no intention of letting her escape so easily, put her in the zoo, and Mrs Conroy found her there and threw all the cages away and cried again. Phoebe did not cry. She went to her father, who asked, 'What can I do to help you, Phoebe?'

'Give me five pounds,' said Phoebe, suddenly remembering something that really would help.

It was not the answer her father had expected, but he tried to understand.

'To buy something for Toby?'

Phoebe shook her head.

'What then?' he asked, wondering if she'd heard talk of funerals at school. 'Flowers for Emma?'

'She's had flowers,' said Phoebe. 'She's had flowers all summer. She still went and died.' Tears were running down Phoebe's cheeks now. 'The mean pig!' said Phoebe.

'Phoebe!'

'You are all mean pigs,' said Phoebe, and stamped upstairs, converted her slipper into a temporary cage and put her father in it.

'I wish their grandmother was here,' said Mr Conroy. 'She might make more sense of them than we can.'

Mrs Conroy said it was just plain naughtiness on Phoebe's part, but when on Tuesday night, Rachel appeared in her parents' bedroom, tear-stained and miserable, and asking not for comfort, as her mother had hoped, but for an advance on their pocket money with no questions asked, she realised it was something more. On Wednesday, when a phone call revealed that Ruth and Naomi had not been at school all week, she remembered Mr Conroy's wise words about their grandmother and rang and asked for help.

That was how, when Ruth, Naomi, Rachel and Phoebe came home on Friday night, an astonishing sight met their eyes. Hands on hips, gazing sternly down the road at them, stood a battered old lady.

'Big Grandma!' they shrieked, and broke into a run.

'Big Grandma indeed!' snapped Big Grandma, as they reached her. 'I think you people have some explaining to do!'

'Oh Big Grandma!' Rachel hugged her round her iron waist.

'Why did you come?' asked Ruth.

'To save your poor mother from madness,' replied Big Grandma. 'Go on, Phoebe! Ask me, I'm waiting. How much?'

'Five pounds, please,' replied Phoebe meekly, 'we've got the other five already.'

Silently Big Grandma handed her the money. Rachel plunged her hand down her front and extracted a jam jar of coins, Naomi dashed inside and returned with an envelope, and Ruth, seizing jam jar, envelope and five pound note, sprinted away round the corner to the Post Office. She returned a few minutes later, out of breath but smiling with relief.

'Happy now?' asked Big Grandma sarcastically, 'or just happy until November? What do you plan to do then?'

'Naomi's birthday's in November,' said Rachel, 'birthday money.'

'Out of interest,' said Big Grandma, 'what would you have done had I'd not turned up this evening and bailed you out?'

'Trick or Treat, or early carol singing,' said Phoebe.

'No we wouldn't,' said Naomi.

'We could have done sledge rides, I thought,' said Rachel, 'only there isn't any snow.'

Ruth and Naomi said nothing.

'I must say,' remarked Big Grandma, 'it's obviously a very good job I came when I did! However, put it all behind you! There's a reception committee waiting to cross-question you indoors.'

'Who?'

'Your mother, as chief (and most indignant) sufferer; your father, home early from work on purpose; Mrs Collingwood in the dual capacity of Emma's solicitor and unwilling victim of your ingenuity, one of many I might add; and myself as interested bystander!'

'Now what have we done?' demanded Naomi.

'You may well ask,' said Big Grandma.

'I haven't done anything wrong for ages,' said Rachel.

'No, neither have I,' protested Phoebe, as she was propelled inside. 'There's nothing wrong with putting people in zoos when they act like they're friends and then go and die.'

'My poor sausage!' said Mrs Collingwood, hearing this remark and catching sight of Phoebe's unhappy face. 'My poor sausage, come here!'

Rachel, who had rushed upstairs for her sledge, came back into the room, holding it like a shield and remarked, 'No one calls me a poor sausage, and I haven't done anything wrong, except what other people made me do and I did it to be kind, and now I'm in trouble! I don't think it's fair!' She positioned her sledge like a wall and got down behind it.

'Nobody is in trouble,' Mrs Conroy said. 'Well, that's not true. You've all been very silly. Why on earth didn't you tell us about this boy in Africa?'

'How do you know about him?' Ruth and Naomi spoke together.

'Your grandmother seems to have guessed a lot,' replied their mother, 'and anyway, Emma told Mrs Collingwood.'

'Emma told?' asked Phoebe furiously. 'Good job she's dead then, I say!'

'Phoebe!' exclaimed Mrs Conroy, and then, seeing the tears running down Phoebe's face, put an arm round her.

'Oh well,' said Ruth bravely, 'it was all my fault. We couldn't tell you at first because I put that I was eighteen when I wasn't. And then we did other things to get the money that we couldn't tell you either . . .'

'Only robbing the Post Office once,' said Rachel sulkily.

'And selling sandwiches made in a dog kennel,' said Mrs Conroy, 'and being street artists, for goodness sake! And you should never have tried to sell those books, Naomi, and you knew it. And poor Mrs Collingwood, Ruth. It's very irresponsible to teach babies bad habits!'

'I didn't want him to grow up too quickly,' said Ruth, 'so that he wouldn't need me to look after him any more, because I needed the money for Joseck.'

'We couldn't charge Toby and Emma, you see,' said Naomi. 'We thought at first we could, but soon we couldn't. They were too kind.'

'Kind!' growled Phoebe. 'Emma told!'

'Emma had to tell me,' explained Mrs Collingwood, 'because I was her solicitor . . .'

'And because she's . . .'

'Hang on, Phoebe,' said Mrs Collingwood, 'because I was her solicitor and she wanted to give some money to your friend in Kenya . . .'

'Emma hadn't got any money,' said Ruth. 'Neither has Toby. They're as poor as poor; you should see where they live.'

'Toby and Emma asked to see me,' continued Mrs Collingwood patiently, 'and because you'd been their friends and given them such a lovely summer, and they knew you needed money. Emma and Toby have, had I should say, although Toby still has of course, quite a lot of money. They sold a farm, you know. But they never had children and they were very lonely. It made a lot of difference you being there and making such friends with them. You stopped them feeling so old.'

'Being old isn't any excuse for anything,' said Phoebe, 'especially sneaking!'

'Emma asked to see me not very long ago,' Mrs Collingwood continued, 'and I helped her make a new will, where she left enough money to see Joseck through his school years and to start him off a little afterwards. She said she owed you that much for the summer in the garden.'

Great silence fell.

It lasted for a long time; longer than any silence that had ever happened in that crowded house.

'Enough for Joseck to stay at school?' asked Naomi, at last, and she looked at Ruth, and Ruth looked at her, and suddenly they also had tears rolling down their cheeks.

'Is it true?' whispered Rachel.

'Is that why she sneaked?' asked Phoebe.

'Yes, it's true and that's why she sneaked,' Mrs Collingwood told them, 'so don't be sad, Phoebe; she didn't stop being your friend. That was her way of helping you. And . . .'

She paused, and then went on. 'She left a little bit of money for you girls, too.'

'For us?'

'For adventures,' she said. 'Emma liked adventures. She told me she was one of the first . . .'

'Girl Guides,' said Ruth, half smiling, half crying. 'Does Toby know all this?'

'Yes.'

'Can he come here at Christmas so he's not on his own?' asked Naomi.

'What a good idea,' said her father.

'He might like Peter,' said Ruth. 'Peter might make him laugh.' She looked hopefully at Mrs Collingwood, who said at once, 'You can introduce them, Ruth, as soon as ever you like.'

'Joseck wants to be a doctor,' said Rachel.

'Perhaps Emma's help will make that easier for him now,' said Mrs Conroy. 'Emma, and you girls. You silly girls . . . not always silly . . . Tea!' she said, suddenly, 'I'll make some tea,' and she blew her nose in the kitchen.

Ruth also jumped to her feet. 'We've got his photograph,' she said, and went to fetch it, and the letters too, and Naomi followed after her and came back with the atlas and all the books about Africa they kept borrowing from the library.

'Tomorrow I must write to him,' said Mrs Collingwood. 'And to his parents as well.'

'So will we,' said Ruth, 'and one day, perhaps . . .'

'We can visit,' said Phoebe, 'and see Mari, and all the goats on the roof.'

'I'll take my sledge,' said Rachel, nodding.

'There's a bus from Nairobi that goes right past the school,' remembered Naomi. 'But we'd have to get passports, and anyway we can't go now, we've got to look after Toby.'

'And Peter,' said Mrs Collingwood, smiling at Ruth.

'And go back to school,' said Big Grandma. 'And try and learn a little sense!'

'Yes, but one day,' said Ruth, 'Martin won't have to wait the bus for us, and the driver won't have to grumble and Egg-Yolk Wendy will be struck dumb with shock because we'll have gone to have adventures. Proper real adventures, like the sort they have in books.'

My friends Ruth, Naomi, Rachel and Phoebe,
I am so happy . . .

Turn the page for an extract from
The Exiles in Love

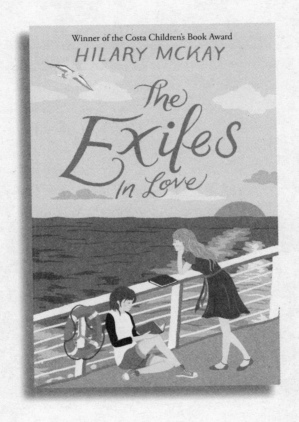

Winner of the Costa Children's Book Award

HILARY McKAY

The Exiles in Love

CHAPTER ONE

Ruth was the eldest of the Conroy girls. In a few weeks' time she would be fifteen. 'I used to think that fifteen would be nearly grown up,' said her sister Naomi, 'until you started being it.' Ruth knew exactly what she meant; she felt the same way herself and she thought the strangest thing about being so old was the fact that it made no difference at all. She was no more self-confident, or organised, or magically in charge of her emotions than she had been in the past. Nothing had changed; she was the same muddle-headed person she had always been, forever swinging between happiness and despair, never doing the right thing at quite the right moment. Naomi, eighteen months younger and two years behind her at school, had far more common sense.

Naomi was brainy, and a much more private person than Ruth. While Ruth either dreamed of miracles or expected the worst, Naomi took a more detached view of life. She and Ruth were very good allies; they understood each other. They read the same books, liked the same friends, detested the same enemies and managed to share a bedroom and yet remain on speaking terms most of the time. They endured with courage their little sisters Rachel and Phoebe.

'Although they really are insane,' remarked Ruth gloomily.

'Don't be silly!' said her mother, although secretly thinking that Ruth had a point. 'Phoebe has been top of her class since the day she started school!'

'That's got nothing to do with whether she's bonkers or not,' observed Naomi.

'And Rachel's teacher says she is a "good average",' continued Mrs Conroy. 'And should be encouraged.'

Rachel was ten. Her latest preoccupation was What They Ate in Books. She had dreams of munching her way through literature.

'After all, it's really quite an original approach to reading!' said Mrs Jones, Rachel's class teacher, at the annual parents' evening. 'And it can't be easy for her. All those clever sisters, not to mention Phoebe coming up behind!'

Mrs Conroy sighed a little.

'I wish I had more ordinary daughters,' she remarked. 'I should never have taught them to read so early.'

'Early reading is an absolutely splendid achievement!' Mrs Jones assured her. 'Absolutely splendid! Dramatically broadens their horizons!'

Mrs Conroy went home and looked at her daughters. Their horizons seemed dramatically narrow. There was Ruth, dripping with tears over *Little Women* (which she must have read a hundred times before). There was Naomi, droning aloud snatches of the poems of Housman.

'I'm sure they're not suitable for a girl of thirteen,' protested Mrs Conroy.

'Thirteen and a half,' said Naomi, 'and school think they're suitable. We did the "cherry hung with snow" one in English literature before the teacher ran away with the French assistant. Listen!' And she read aloud with great enjoyment:

'Before this fire of sense decay,
This smoke of thought blow clean away,
And leave with ancient night alone,
The steadfast and enduring bone.'

'Very morbid and exaggerated and I'm sure you can't understand a word of it!' said Mrs Conroy, and turned away, and there was Phoebe, who at the age of eight read nothing but stories where teenage girl sleuths drove beautiful cars and wore mysterious dark glasses and never had to go to school.

Last of all, there was Rachel.

'Not bonkers!' Mrs Conroy told herself firmly.

'What's fat salt pork?' asked Rachel, looking up from her book. 'They seem to eat a lot of it here.'

She held up *Little House on the Prairie* to show the book she meant.

'They eat it with beans,' she continued. 'How was the parents' evening? Did Mrs Jones say nice things about me?'

'Why ever shouldn't she?' asked Mrs Conroy evasively.

*

189

Rachel and Phoebe both went to the same junior school. Ruth and Naomi attended the local comprehensive, travelling by school bus. It was just on the point of leaving for home one April afternoon when Ruth, tearstained, dishevelled and breathless, scrabbled aboard.

'Don't tell me you've had cookery again,' remarked Naomi, as Ruth flopped down beside her, and she regarded her sister's wicker cookery basket with suspicion and disgust. 'We've only just got through the last lot.'

Ruth didn't reply. She sat silently clutching her basket, hunched against the motion of the bus.

'If it's more fish pie,' said Naomi, 'I can't bear it. I shall turn vegetarian like Phoebe.'

Waste not, want not was a very firm policy in the Conroy household. If it was food, it was eaten, and that was that. So far the results of Ruth's cookery lessons had been counted as food.

'It isn't anything like that,' said Ruth, holding her basket even more tightly and fumbling in her blazer pocket for something to wipe her nose on.

Naomi raised a corner of the basket's plastic cover, peered inside, and then jumped back in alarm.

'What on earth is it?' she demanded. 'It looks like a squashed hedgehog!'

'Leave it alone!' snapped Ruth.

'It was Simple Cottage Rolls today,' someone from Ruth's class told Naomi helpfully.

The smell that had arisen from Ruth's basket when Naomi

lifted the cover was not that of simple cottage rolls. It was a sweetish, rankish, rancidish smell. A hedgehoggy smell.

'Let me look again,' said Naomi. 'Let me look properly. It's only fair if I've got to eat it.'

Ruth gave in. After all, Naomi would have to know sometime or other. Gently she uncovered the contents of her basket enough to allow her sister to look again.

It was a squashed hedgehog.

'Don't frighten it,' said Ruth.

'Isn't it dead, then?'

'Of course not. It's just curled up. But a car's hit it; there's blood on some of its spines. I found it in the gutter by the school gates.'

'When?'

'Afternoon break.'

'Where's it been since then?'

'In my cookery basket.'

'What did you do with the rolls you made, then?'

'Chucked them away.'

'Well, that's something,' said Naomi with relief.

The whole bus had been quiet while people eavesdropped on this conversation, but now it erupted into a torrent of noise. Squashed hedgehog jokes were called from seat to seat and there were loud predictions about the agility and appetite of the invalid's fleas. Ruth was assailed by shouts of advice, compliments on the sudden improvement of her cooking skills, squeals of disgust and wails of sympathy. Wendy, the girl who always knew everything, hung over the back of her seat to tell them the name of a vet to whom she had once taken a squashed hedgehog herself.

'He did it for me free,' she said.

'Did what?' demanded Naomi.

'Put it to sleep.'

'Should you have wrapped it in your jumper?' asked Martin-the-good, leaning across the aisle to peer over Ruth's shoulder.

'Anyone started itching yet?' enquired a voice from the back of the bus, and was answered by shrieks and hoots from all sides. Two people fell scratching and writhing into the aisle. The noise reached a crescendo.

Ruth, unable to bear it any longer, thrust the basket into Naomi's arms, and was preparing to leap to her feet and do battle when everyone suddenly cannoned forward as the bus jerked to a halt.

'ENOUGH!' roared the driver, blasting his passengers into silence. 'PACK IT IN!'

Limp with astonishment and relief, Ruth stared at him in admiration. He was new that term, and she'd never really noticed him before, but now she thought that no knight in shining armour ever made a more welcome rescue.

'Crikey!' said the bus driver in an ordinary voice, and drove on.

Once Ruth was off the bus and on home ground, the reactions to the contents of her cookery basket were slightly better.

'Oh, you wrapped it in your jumper!' said Mrs

Collingwood, the Conroys' next-door neighbour and mother of Martin-the-good, but she added, 'Poor little thing!'

'You ought not to have wrapped it in your jumper!' said Ruth's mother. 'Still, I suppose it will wash. Put it in the shed and leave it in peace and we'll see how it is after supper.'

'Olden days people used to eat hedgehogs,' remarked Rachel through a mouthful of macaroni cheese. 'Covered in mud and baked in their jackets.'

'Shut up!' said Ruth.

'I think that was cruel,' continued Rachel. 'Their poor little prickles cooking!'

'Shut up!' said Ruth.

'No worse than eating sheep,' Phoebe pointed out. 'Or cows. Or pigs. Or horses.'

'I don't eat horses,' protested Rachel.

'They do in France,' said Phoebe. 'I expect you would if you were there.'

After supper there was a worried hedgehog inspection.

'It will have to see a vet,' said Ruth at last. 'How much do you think it will cost?'

'Wendy said it was free.'

'That was just for putting down. I want this one making better.'

'Ask when you telephone,' suggested Naomi.

Unfortunately when Ruth telephoned she found that the nearest vet was closed for the day. So was the next nearest. So was the next nearest, which was twelve miles away and not near at all. Ruth left messages on all three answerphones, describing (with sobs) the extremeness of the emergency, but carefully not mentioning the species of animal involved. This was a precaution in case a hedgehog wouldn't be considered important enough to deserve an after-hours visit.

'Don't you think it's a bit much,' asked Naomi, 'calling out three vets to one squashed hedgehog? What will Mum say if they all turn up together in the middle of the night?'

'What else could I do?' asked Ruth. 'She'll know I had to. She won't mind.'

'I bet she will.'

'I'll find out,' said Rachel, and before she could be stopped had dashed into the kitchen. A moment later they could hear her breathlessly enquiring, 'Do you mind that Ruth has telephoned three midnight vets to come and see her hedgehog?'

'What do you mean?'

'She told them on their answerphones that it was life or death. She said you wouldn't mind.'

'Ruth! You couldn't have been so silly!' exclaimed Mrs Conroy, hurrying out of the kitchen.

'Why is it silly?' asked Ruth, still sniffing. 'What else could I do?'

'Sometimes,' said Mrs Conroy crossly, 'you behave more like four than fourteen! For goodness' sake go back and look up their numbers and cancel them, Naomi. Rachel, I saw you! Come out of the fridge! You've had your supper! And where has Phoebe vanished to just at bedtime?'

'She's gone next door,' said Rachel, through a handful of

hastily grabbed cheese. 'Practising her spying and sleuthing, I expect.'

'You girls go from one silly phase to another!' said Mrs Conroy. 'Go and fetch her, someone, and apologise to Mrs Collingwood if she's been rude . . . not you, Rachel!'

But Rachel had already gone, chewing as she went. She liked Mrs Collingwood, who always asked if she was hungry, and Martin-the-good (who she was planning to marry if the worst came to the worst), and Martin's little brother Peter, who saved his biscuit ends for her, and Josh, the next-door dog, and most of all she liked apologising for her sisters, especially Phoebe, who was often difficult to keep squashed into her proper place as the youngest of the family.

'Mum says she's sorry if Phoebe's been rude,' she told Mrs Collingwood smugly.

'Rude?' asked Mrs Collingwood. 'Phoebe?'

'Spying,' explained Rachel.

'Spying!' Mrs Collingwood laughed. 'She's been unloading the dishwasher, good as gold!'

'Oh,' said Rachel, very disappointed. 'Well, anyway, it's her bedtime.'

Phoebe said goodnight to the Collingwoods and went with Rachel very meekly, but on the street outside she remarked, 'Do you know what happens to people who blow other people's cover?'

'What?' asked Rachel.

'I'll lend you a book,' said Phoebe.

Read them all

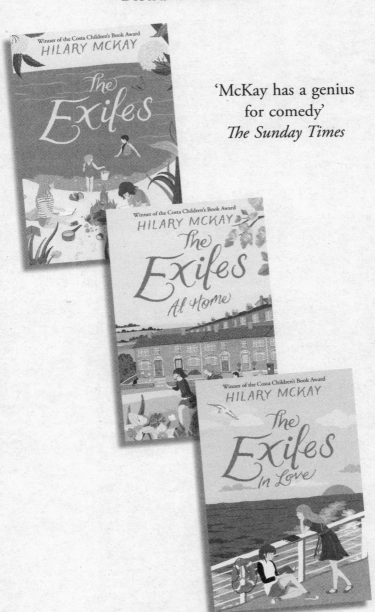

'McKay has a genius
for comedy'
The Sunday Times

ABOUT THE AUTHOR

Hilary McKay is a critically-acclaimed author who has won many awards, including the Costa Children's Book Award 2018 for *The Skylarks' War*, the *Guardian* Children's Fiction Prize for her first novel, *The Exiles*, and the Whitbread (now the Costa) Award for *Saffy's Angel*.

The Exiles are inspired by Hilary's own childhood growing-up as one of four sisters, and the second book in the trilogy, *The Exiles at Home*, was the winner of the Smarties Prize.

Hilary studied Botany and Zoology at the University of St Andrews, and worked as a biochemist before the draw of the pen became too strong and she decided to become a full-time writer. She lives in Derbyshire with her family.

COMING SOON

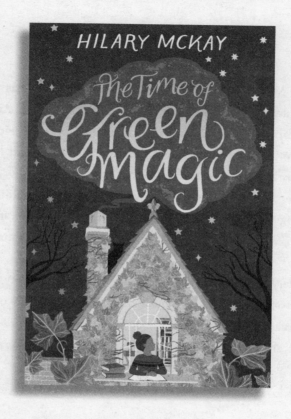

A beautiful, spell-binding novel about new families, a magical old house and a mysterious visitor, from acclaimed author and Costa-winner, Hilary McKay